This story is a sequel to the novels, *THE BEST ACTRESS* when actress Nicole Bennett goes to L.A....and *BLUE HARBOUR REVISITED*. A novel about when Nicole visits Sir Noel Coward's home in [illegible]ca.

In praise of "Passionate Pilgrim[illegible]ard" Welcome Rain Publishers. ISBN 9[illegible]

"Elizabeth Sharland will squire you to places you never thought you'd go, in impeccable language and with rare grace. Learn, then, how George Sand whiled away the hours with Chopin at Chateau de Nohant, and spend some time with Somerset Maugham at Cap Ferrat near Nice. Katherine Mansfield charms us in Menton, alongside Franco Zeffirelli in Positano, Italy, Cole Porter in Paris, Paul Bowles in Morocco and Lady Gregory in Ireland. The illustrations are lavish, offering visual clues to the geniuses that inhabit these pages. Travel with Sharland as you have never traveled before. A blessing on your cranium."

MALACHY McCOURT

In praise of "Behind the Doors of Notorious Covent Garden." ISBN 978-1-401-8498-7

"Elizabeth is a musician, artists, pianist, a traveler and a playwright.... who better to guide us around Covent Garden?"

HUGO VICKERS. *The Unexpurgated Beaton: The Cecil Beaton Diaries.*

On The Riviera

by Elizabeth Sharland

a novel

iUniverse, Inc.
Bloomington

On The Riviera
A Novel

iUniverse books may be ordered through booksellers or by contacting:

iUniverse
1663 Liberty Drive
Bloomington, IN 47403
www.iuniverse.com
1-800-Authors (1-800-288-4677)

ISBN: 978-1-4502-8151-5 (sc)
ISBN: 978-1-4502-8152-2 (ebook)
ISBN: 978-1-4502-8153-9 (dj)

Printed in the United States of America

iUniverse rev. date: 1/07/2011

Dedicated to Lydia and Alan

Chapter One

Sitting on the terrace of the Carlton Hotel in Cannes I thought how ironic it is to be here again. At least it wasn't crowded and noisy as it was the last time I was here, during the Film Festival when the whole place was madness.

The events remembered from my past visit to Cannes are still very vivid. However that is one of the reasons I have come back here, to lay the ghost.

Last week in London, when I told my agent he looked at me as if I was insane. "There are very few examples of actors who give up their careers, their passion, their reason for living, to write a book in the south of France!" How true! I didn't even know if I could write! Maybe I was insane, or very stupid. But, you see, I had already lost the love of my life, Michael, a brilliant writer, tall and blonde like Peter O'Toole, because of my devotion to acting, and my career. I left him for six months to do a film in Los Angeles and he met someone else while I was gone, and now it looks as if I have messed up my life again, in a different way.

The phrase "But that was another time, and in another country," springs to mind. Who wrote that? Two years ago I was here for two days with my first film and where I first met Michael. We arrived for the press reception, a company party, and the showing of the film the next evening then we left in the brilliant golden sunshine of the early morning back to the gray skies of London. It was then that I promised myself two days is not enough to discover the beauty of the Riviera, and now especially now, I wanted to think things over about leaving England.

How do people do it? One day, they decide to uproot and change their lives, go to another country, change their careers, throw out possessions, they just go and do it which sometimes turns out to be a brilliant idea, other times, not. We know the risks and we know the ramifications of doing such things.

Years ago, my childhood dream had come true, beyond all expectations really, to become a successful actress playing great characters. I was still in my early thirties then. That was long ago and now it is over. I have officially retired. The scripts were not great, the effort of getting up at 4 am every morning was really awful and I was tired. I have looped the looped and given it all up. Why keep on acting roles that were so repetitive and gave no artistic satisfaction or sense of achievement, at all. I wanted to create something of my own, and I certainly have burnt all my bridges to do so. I am determined not to regret anything.

It is a lovely cool evening in early summer. The soft warm breeze very gently ripples through the row of palm trees, along the Croisette, through the colorful flowers beds everywhere and the striped umbrellas. The air reminds one of what it must have been like in Shakespeare's A Midsummer Night's Dream in that it seems magical, full of spirits, expectation, deep wonderment of the very stuff that dreams are made of. Magical, almost mystical, it conjures up the exact description of the setting. It is twilight, dusk, and the light on the Riviera is truly memorable. That's why so many painters make their way down here. The air, the light, the colors, the skies are unique to this area. It makes me feel buoyant, alive, expectant of I know not what.

This is the place that I instinctively, physically and spiritually really want to be. Guy de Maupassant wrote that he found the south of France inspirational. "I am in a dream. The first traces of spring here tug at my nature and pull out literary fruits that I didn't know were there." He stayed for seven years.

Usually your life ambitions start very early, this one of mine, came later but it is just as strong.

After finding a place to live in a small *pension* I decided to spend sometime acclimatizing myself before beginning to write, or more appropriately, trying to write. That was one week ago. I wanted to change my life, totally change my life. The trouble is I get very restless and I must try taking each day as it comes.

The waiter brings a glass of Kir with some delicious plump green olives and some salty, slightly oily golden crisps served in a little silver dish. As I sit here, ruminating, it is a fine place to ruminate, looking out across the water, watching the breathtaking beautiful sunset I notice the fantastic shadows, they are much darker than shadows elsewhere. Almost black. The whole scene just knocks you out. Another quote comes to mind "if you are tired of life"...ah yes, well we all know that's about London of course, however what about Wordworth's poem about standing on that bridge in London... but if you are tired of this beautiful scene then you are really tired of life. In London now, you could complain that the view from the bridge has been totally destroyed by the new view of the London skyline. St.Paul's almost blocked out by those huge new skyscrapers. You remember things that used to be beautiful and no longer are; the longer you live the more memories of such things, you have. That view used to be sensational with St. Paul's and many old church steeples dominating the skyline. No longer, those buildings block them out. Too late now.

There is something about being by the Mediterranean. I still remember and still feel the initial impact, there is such ancient history connected with this sea. Even more so in Greece. The beginning of European civilization, the legends, the profound beauty of the place, all gives a kind of solace for the soul.

Obviously there are changes in one's appearance over the years, but I hoped mine had been minimal. My blonde hair is long again, I am still too short, have put on ten pounds but at least I've taken a huge step toward a new life. Hopefully I have made the right decision, to leave everything behind, everything, and try and become a full time writer. I felt elated and the Kir was making me believe I have done the right thing. However most of the writers who had lived down here had been married or had a companion living with them, not many seem to have lived alone. I hadn't reckoned on loneliness. I felt very lonely, even though I was usually very self-reliant.

Sipping the Kir, I thought of the time when I was working with Yul Brynner in the *King and I.* One day I was surprised to hear him say that "you are really alone in this world, and if anybody can help you along the way, then be very grateful." It was surprising at the time because he was newly married and had dozens of close friends, many of whom used to come backstage after the show at one time or another to congratulate him. Hundreds of fans wrote to him each week, and he was regarded as some kind of super hero when it was announced that he had beaten cancer, which of course was not true.

The view was fabulous and the sunset was just beginning, if only I had someone to share it with.

Last week back in rainy Oxford, I had left Nigel, my new husband. He is a handsome British businessman, with lovely brown curly hair, deep tan, blue eyes, thin, and very attractive. I had met him while on holiday in Jamaica. It had been a whirlwind romance; I was still recovering from Michael and he was mourning his wife, who had died recently. He had no idea where I was, or at least I didn't think he knew. We had been married nearly a year, but we had a huge problem and a row dealing with his son from his former marriage. It immediately showed me very clearly, that he was more involved with his son, than with me. So I had left him to try to find a new life on my own. It seemed the only thing to do.

A few weeks before, I had been very influenced by a book by fellow actor, Dirk Bogarde. The book stirred something deep within me. The possibility of a new life. The book was a volume of his letters, and in one letter he writes of the anguish of deciding about his career. He wrote that he was fed up with acting in what he called, 'crap pictures' and that he thought that personal happiness is worth far more than fame and fortune. The sense of living a life that you really want and the sense of achievement it brings, is the most important thing in life.

In one of his letters to a friend he writes 'Writing is a new land, unwalked, full of strange paths through the peat, heather and bogs of despair. I'm having to teach myself to write. It's difficult.'

Years ago when I was just starting out, I was invited to one of his 'Sunday lunches' at his great manor house "Nore" deep in the lush English countryside. I had been terribly impressed with the house and the people who were there. They were all stars of the West End then and table talk was all theatre, films, directors, scripts, who was traveling where and when. He was warm, witty and I completely fell in love with him. Why is it that the timing of reading a certain book can change your life? My father went to Greece soon after reading *The Odyssey* for example. He studied Greek mythology for the rest of his life.

When Dirk died a few years ago, it was a terrific shock and I mourned him. I still do. He was a one-of-a-kind person, complicated, talented, private, a wonderful actor, and later on a terrific writer.

His book "An Orderly Man" is about his move to live in the south of France, and he wrote several more about the subject. He made it seem the most romantic thing to do ever. He writes of the supreme joy and happiness he felt after he had bought a house just nearby Cannes. However his fears about buying a 500-year-old farm house, were soon confirmed. Had he known that the "400 old olive trees on the land, had been neglected for more than 30 years and were slowly dying, that the sparkling springs from which he drank so romantically, came not from the bowels of Provence, but from the leaks in the giant reservoir for Cannes, high in the hill behind him. The bramble and broom concealed acres of once tilled land on which had grown jasmine, roses and artichokes."

Suddenly I became aware of a man sitting at the next table, his chair back was resting along my chair back. I turned around to him, to ask if we could separate the chairs slightly. He smiled and looked lonely. So I repeated the request, and he answered and smiled again, moving his chair slightly back.

"Of course."

"It is a magnificent sunset isn't it?" I said, returning his smile.

We started talking across the tables to one another. The weather, the forecast, the traffic, the usual things. The wine was hitting me. Then he said,

"If you are alone, why don't you join me?" Obviously he hadn't recognized me, thank goodness.

"Why not? If I am not intruding." I picked up my glass and sat in the chair at the next table. And so I met Henry.

"Hi, my name is Nicole Bennett."

"Hullo, I'm Henry Morehead."

"Do you come here often?" we both smiled at the cliché. How often I had used it in jest. It has got me into lots of trouble over the years.

"Yes. Practically every night. I haven't seen you here before." he smiled.

"I haven't been in Cannes for very long. I'm not staying here I'm in a small *pension* down the road. However I know this terrace well."

He had no idea who I was, even though I had just told him my name. I liked that, because I knew we could have a more normal conversation. Some actors would be offended but I realized a long time ago, that it is better not to be recognized. The questions are all the same.

He was around fifty I guessed. Rather stocky, well dressed, round faced with a bushy but well trimmed moustache, thinning brown hair, a brown Harris Tweed jacket, he spoke with an Oxbridge accent. A soft-spoken man, well educated who seemed to be enjoying the view as much as I was.

"I live in Cannes, and I usually came here with my wife. But she died several weeks ago and I haven't been out very much these days." He teared up and for a moment I thought he was going to cry.

"Oh dear, I'm very sorry to hear that." I had to change the subject fast, or any more sympathy probably would start him off.

He needed some kind of distraction, as he probably had been at home all day, grieving. I knew all about that, and will never forget it. Clearing out clothes, papers, everything. Awful times. When my mother died and I was totally overwhelmed with grief, guilt, and remorse, especially when I had to do all the clearing out of her closets, possessions, and papers and discover all the times she must have been so very lonely. He must be busy doing the same kind of things day after day.

"How long have you lived in Cannes?" I smiled again.

"Over two years. We retired to Bournemouth, but we grew tired of that and the bitter cold, so as we both loved France, we sold up and bought a flat down here. It is not far from here. We were both teachers, and we both were Francophiles. We'd been here many times before on our holidays and always said we would retire here."

It wasn't difficult to imagine how hard they must have worked as teachers and the dreary grind of correcting essays and marking papers. The freezing winters and the snotty little kids with their wet uniforms drying out in the warm classroom. The discipline, the homework, the constant stress of dealing with sometimes cheeky and insolent kids made me admire their tenacity. The idea that both of them used to teach was quite amazing. What lives. What tedious work even though it probably was rewarding when students did well and remembered you years later, which was a kind of reward I suppose. Most people remember the name of their first grade teacher years later.

"A good idea. Don't you miss teaching and your work back home?"

"I try to write and send some articles back to the local paper. I know the editor and he sometimes publishes them. They keep me going."

Later on, after a second drink, he opened up a little and explained what had happened to him.

"We were driving along the Croisette one morning and my wife suddenly said she had a splitting, blinding headache and would have to stop the car. She had decided to drive that day unfortunately. Well, she pulled over, and then the next thing that happened was that she fell heavily against me. I turned to her and saw that she was dead. Her eyes were open and she had stopped breathing.'

"How shocking. What ever did you do?"

"Somehow I managed to get into the driver's seat and drive to the hospital. It was too late of course; there was nothing they could do. She was gone."

It was like hearing that someone had been hit crossing the road or had been killed in a thunderstorm, you just can't take it in. I had been through it all, the shock and the loss when my mother died.

He turned to me, "How about you? What brings you here?"

He looked me in the eyes, as if he wanted to stop talking about what he had just told me. It was too recent, too painful.

It was up to me to change the subject and relieve him of reliving that experience.

"Oh nothing as sad as that. Just a bit of a shock really. I've only been married for a year, and we have just split up. I think it's final because we really don't have much past history. But I hope you don't mind I'd rather not talk about it, just now."

"Of course, I understand. If you ever need to, don't hesitate." He picked up his drink.

We sat there talking about our early school days, of all things, anything to distract him from the trauma that was still so fresh in his mind. The sun had gone down and it was getting dark

"I've come here to try and write a book."

"That's interesting. What about?" he asked.

"The writers who have lived down here in the past, and the ones that are still here. You know, it's strange but some of them are viewed as such romantic figures, the Murphys and the Scott Fitzgeralds, for example, appeared to have lived a golden life, but in actual fact, their lives later on were full of tragedy and despair."

There was a pause. An angel passed.

"Please would you have dinner with me? It is good to talk to someone. Usually I just go home and fix myself something out of a tin, but you are such good company, we could have a simple meal somewhere. I have a few restaurants I go to, down in the old town. Have you other plans?"

"No I don't. But let's make it a dutch treat shall we?" I thought he might be asking me out of politeness and may not have that much money. I thought that it might help me too to have some company.

We walked down the Croisette to the old town square. There are many reasonably priced bistros down there, serving delicious local dishes and good local wine. This particular restaurant had the best soup au Pistou I had ever tasted. It was full of fresh vegetables, spiced with garlic and herbs de provence, it was sensational. We followed that with a hot, crispy golden roasted chicken breast, baked potatoes covered in the lightest cheese and onion sauce with tiny green peas and carrots, straight from the market that morning. The crème brulée was worthy of the best restaurant in Paris. I relished the food not only because it was so good but also because I was hungry. It was a great comfort as it often is when you are stressed out and wonder what you can do. My appetite had returned since coming to France and I knew I would have to be careful if I didn't want to pile on more pounds.

"They say that you can never go back." I blurted out. "I don't know who said it actually, but I think you can go back, that is to some places at least. Those good times in the past may not have been so good actually. But time makes them seem as if they were good. I can remember trying to sell a film script here once. How ridiculous."

It was a totally stupid thing to try to do but it is strange that you often confide things to complete stranger, things that you wouldn't tell your best friend. Why is that? Maybe because you don't have to worry about their judgments."

He didn't ask too many questions which I appreciated. I really didn't want to talk about myself. Anyway where would I start? First he was talking about his early life, and then we got on to general subjects, mostly to do with settling in France and how to cope with the language that you thought you knew so well.

"Why is it that when you arrive in France, nobody seems to understand your French, or at least unless you repeat it three times over." I asked.

"After a week or so, when you learn the accent and inflections, it is easier. I have a good ear and can adjust to the pronunciations when listening to the person who is speaking to me."

"I'm sure that is why many people give up on the language because nobody understands you at first. Bonjour seems to be the only word that nobody misunderstands."

"It gets better, just keep talking!"

"I remember listening to my teacher at school, and she certainly didn't speak like the locals down here. I never concentrated at school, because I thought it was a language I would never use. Why is it that even though you may master the language brilliantly, you feel that you can never really become a French person, or be taken for one."

"You have to have been born here." He laughed.

"When I was a teenager, I had this ambition of wanting to live in every capital city in the world. Don't ask me why! However I haven't done too badly so far. I've lived in London, Paris, New York, Los Angeles, Sydney and now I'm here. This is really far more beautiful than living in any city."

"Thank goodness, not many people realize that fact."

"The trick is to keep busy. I get bored very easily."

A cool breeze had suddenly started so we got up to leave. He insisted on paying the bill, and we settled that I would pay next time.

The wine had helped him relax; he took my arm as we walked back the same way we had come. It was a friendly gesture, a comforting one. It turned out his flat was quite close to the place where I was staying. I told him I wanted to try and write a book and I knew he wanted to ask me more questions but it was late.

"There were so many writers who lived down here and wrote about it I would love to experience the life they lead down here and write about it. Not just people like the Murphys and Scott Fitzgerald, but all the others. I don't expect a life of luxury, with wild parties and craziness. I've already had that." I wondered what he would think of that statement.

"Is there any place you would like to visit here? I have a car, and we could drive somewhere for lunch if you like."

"Well yes, actually. There is. I really want to visit St.Paul de Vence because it was one village I had always missed." He suggested he drive me up there the next day, without hesitation, which I thought was rather nice.

"I have the car parked in the garage but I just haven't used it since my wife died. I think I can use it now, especially if I have someone with me. I don't really enjoy driving."

"I love to drive. Please let me, I really want to get to know this area."

"It's all settled then."

"Yes, I'd love to do that."

"Then come around to my place around ten and we'll leave early."

He shook my hand as we parted at the end of the street. "Till tomorrow then." He looked happier, thank goodness.

Walking back to my little *pension*, I looked forward to seeing a village I had read about for years, and remembered it was one of Dirk's favorite places. The place was supposed to be heaven. I wanted to see for myself.

Now at last I was doing something towards gathering material for my book. It was almost a passion to discover the places where these writers lived and to meet new friends. People who stimulate you in mind, body and soul! I couldn't wait! And to discover places that you will remember all your life. Where else but on the Riviera?

Chapter Two

Next morning I walked around to Henry's building. It was a modern block just behind the tennis courts that were just behind the Majestic Hotel. I pressed the front door buzzer and he clicked open the door. Walking down the corridor to his flat, I had a few qualms about visiting him there. I had no idea what to expect. I didn't think it would be a dump but what if he tried to jump on my bones or make suggestions, I didn't think so. I was right, he was a perfect gentleman.

The flat was rather nicely furnished and he gave me a short tour of the two bedrooms. There were photos presumably of his wife on various pieces of furniture; she was standing by a boat, or at the beach, two of them together somewhere, a whole life together. It wasn't good manners to look too closely. Her presence was there, and the photos were just a reminder, as if one was needed. How long it would be before he would put them away. The place was well kept and tidy, with no dirty dishes in the sink. There were plenty of books, although there wasn't time to look at any titles to see what he liked to read, but there were tall bookcases in the living room and bedrooms. The kitchen was modern and there was a nice view of people playing tennis from the window. I must check those courts out I thought, it has been ages since I played.

He locked up and we walked down to the basement garage to get his car. I suggested that I drive as I knew he didn't want to, so we got in, the car started right away, and he directed me out through the exit and up on to the road that lead to St.Paul.

We had planned to leave early because we'd heard of the hordes of tourist buses that have now discovered the village and ruined the peaceful town square where you used to be able to see Yves Montand playing Boules with the locals. He was a local himself, and he and Simone Signoret made their home there, way back in the days before the whole place was 'discovered.'

During the drive up into the hills, I started a rather long explanation telling Henry all about meeting Dirk years ago. Fortunately he remembered him and admired him, so he was pleased to hear about his experiences and settling down here. He realized my enthusiasm for coming down here was partly because having given up my career, I wanted to be sure that I had done the right thing. Just as I had once wanted to be a successful actress, when I first met Dirk, now I wanted to become a writer, and live here in the area where he had lived. For inspiration, I suppose.

He wrote about the fantastic 'light' of the Riviera. He loved the views, the skies, the landscape. In one of his books he wrote that the view from the top of the steps at the Hotel du Cap, looking over the sea to the Esterel mountains in the distance, was absolutely breathtaking, and if anyone didn't agree, then they weren't worthy of breathing.

I had been to the local library to get books by other writers who had lived and worked in this part of the world. All the books written by Bogarde of course, I'd already read. His writing seemed so effortless, as if he just sat down and dashed off a chapter whenever he felt like it. Then there were his letters, collected and edited by John Coldstream who also wrote his biography. Both volumes were in the library and it was with a rush of pleasure that I checked them out. But I quickly learnt that from those two books, just how difficult Bogarde found writing to be. He kept writing to his editor saying he was struggling every day. Yet, one would never think he had a problem at all. His letters are witty and bitchy sometimes but so descriptive. It is as if you are there in his studio, a former olive storage room, experiencing the dreaded mistral, the rain storms, the spring blossom, and discovering how much he loved gardening and his garden. Half the time, he was outside gardening, and planting things, pruning, dead heading, lawn mowing and keeping the very large terraced garden in shape. He writes that as he aged it became more and more difficult. He hired a gardener, a little Arab named Ahmet who kept making 'atrocious things in cement and stone' and which Dirk was always trying to cover up with creepers.

He loved the place and entertained very often, with friends staying over sometimes for weeks in the summer. He writes that he seemed to be doing the washing up all the time and was sick to death of it. One wonders why he didn't get a dishwasher. Surely they were available. He had a large television so there must have been enough power supply. Some mystery.

He set his daily quota at 1800 words. That's a lot. I made up my mind to research what other writers set themselves. I thought 800 might be enough, but then it might take two years!

Because his companion, Tony Forwood was in ill health, they had to sell the house after sixteen years there and move back to London. Tony died, and after living on for another eleven years, Dirk died too. His nephew and his wife, brought his ashes back to his house here, and they were scattered in the garden. He loved the place so much, this is where they thought he would want to be. His films and books will remember his career and life, which is fortunate, but as a person he will be remembered like a character out of a novel. A figment in time. A great character, whether it be in fiction or non-fiction. A Dickens type of character that you have conjured up in your head after the writer has so carefully described them, so I suppose a dead person is much the same. If you meet someone you greatly admire when they are still alive, does your expectation and imagination somehow fail in the meeting? Perhaps, only if they say something that shatters your opinion of them.

But what is the difference from a character in a novel, or to someone who is now dead, or someone you never met, the same as someone who you had known? In his letters his love for the south of France is described over and over again, and he was heartbroken when they had to sell the house.

Chapter Three

It was turning out to be a glorious day. The sunshine was superb, the sky was deep cobalt blue and cloudless, forming a wonderful backdrop as we drove by rows of tall dark green cypress trees, lining the road, bright yellow bushes of mimosa, orange trees, and olive groves, old rustic houses and cows looking at us as we passed by. The gum trees with their long leafy branches intertwined with oak trees. The various perfumes reaching us as we drove by, each turn in the road brought a new scene and here and there were signs pointing to little villages that sounded fascinating. There was not much traffic on the road and when we arrived we were lucky to find a parking spot.

We walked through the small village of St. Paul de Vence, looking at the little boutiques and art galleries, scattered along among the tiny alleyways. There were dozens of watercolours, oils, pencil sketches mostly of the village and the surrounding hills. It is a pity that the old place is now just full of shops and souvenirs, although the old buildings still remain and of course, the views.

"Let's have lunch at the Colombe d'Or, outside on the terrace." He smiled.

"That would be lovely" I knew it was expensive but if he suggested it then he must have meant it.

We sat under the fig trees in the courtyard and the whole was heavenly. I remember Dirk writing about the place and details of his first meeting with Simone Signoret there.

The atmosphere is intoxicating, sitting in the shade of the trees with the strong blue speckled shadows, the sun's rays shining on a silver wine bucket or a serving dish.

The setting is so picturesque, almost like an impressionist painting. That glorious golden light falling on the leaves of the trees and the flower boxes that formed a colorful contrast to the gleaming white tablecloths and silverware. The place was very peaceful, in the noonday sun, there was a kind of hushed expectancy and people seem to be very animated, but at the same time slightly subdued, as they waited for their lunch. (Also probably thinking about the bill.) The waiters in their white starched jackets move swiftly between the tables, opening bottles of wine, serving delicious food and carrying on the tradition of a high-class French country restaurant. A real paradise.

Fortunately it seemed off the tourist track, divided by a heavy gate, and the clientele all looked rather posh. I remember as a student traveling through France, almost broke, staying at youth hostels, with no thought of eating at these kinds of places, but envying the people you saw entering them. One day, yes, one day. So I expect that day had come, and I was enjoying it all immensely. How escapist. How simple minded.. I could feel the spirit of all the artists who must have sat just where we were sitting. The story goes that they paid their bills by giving the owners canvases. Later on we found that story to be true, as we went through the hotel lobby and found some masterpieces by famous artists hanging on the thick stone walls within the series of small rooms on the ground floor. There was a photo of Yves Montand sitting by the swimming pool here and again I knew that here there had been fantastic parties with their friends.

Henry insisted on paying so I didn't argue. I knew he could afford it, so I didn't feel so guilty. We drove back in a haze of good food and wine. It had been a lovely outing.

The countryside is so lovely when you get off the main roads, and behind the coast roads.

During the next few weeks, we studied maps and books, then drove around the Riviera, stopping for lunch at little villages, sometimes in very simple bistros, if the view was good. The weather was warm and ideal for eating out doors. I tried to listen to his stories from the past hoping I was helping him recover from his loss. How does anyone know? Sometimes the memory of some you love jumps up at you who you haven't thought of for years, which opens up a new thought that there were so many things you had forgotten. Some detail, a piece of clothing perhaps, or some jewelry, a watchstrap, dark hairs on the back of a hand, or even just a look, suddenly brings it all back.

I started to go to the early morning market in Cannes. Henry encouraged me to go with him, as we began to eat at his place more often. The old market is one of the most colorful places in the town. The fish gleaming in the sun, arrives at dawn, the striped awnings covering the various sea food from the morning heat. Nowhere else have I seen such a variety of shell food, fuzzy balls of various colors and sizes, weird looking fish, oysters, and creatures from the sea that I have never seen before. Huge arrays of flowers, sweet smelling roses, dahlias, daisies, deep purple lilac, bunches of mimosa, tulips and bulbs of every color, lilies, peonies and rows and rows of green plants, and flowering shrubs. The pungent smell of the vegetables and fruit, was delightful. Piles of oranges, lemons, grapefruit, melons, apples, grapes and practically any kind of berry you could want. The lively atmosphere was filled with the cries of the vendors and there was vitality in that morning air, which was infectious. The aroma of fresh roasted coffee and freshly baked croissants coming from the cafes nearby, was irresistible, so we would always stop at one of them for breakfast, watching the scene unfold in front of us. The smell of the flowers was overpowering and it was a time when you realized how ancient the tradition of an open-air market actually is, almost timeless. We would walk back with our canvas trolley heavy with produce, looking forward to sampling what we had bought.

The whole town is full of color. The palm trees, the canvas awnings, the shop windows, whether it be the high priced fashion or the boutiques, the furniture and antique shops, the windows of the art galleries, the hotel gardens or the Croisette itself, it is hard to imagine an English equivalent. The open-air markets in London leave a lot to be desired.

Chapter Four

Lying in bed that night, I started feeling very anxious about this whole adventure. Was I really stupid to be trying to change my life? On the other hand, this place was so beautiful maybe I would never again have the opportunity to try to do this. Suddenly it might be too late. Life doesn't go on forever, and several of my closest friends had died within a year of each other, which really brought home this fact. It's best to do things while you still want to do them.

Earlier in the day, I had asked Henry if he would drive to Menton with me. This was to be an important chapter for my book. It is the last town on the Riviera, before you get to the Italian border. It is here that the writer, Katherine Mansfield lived. Sadly she lived a very short life. Her account of living on the Riviera was vastly different from the Jazz age group.

Up early next morning, I pulled on my white jeans and blue tee shirt, stepped into my leather sandals, put my hair into a pony tail tied with a blue ribbon, and grabbed my camera and sunglasses.

Then after some orange juice, croissants and coffee, we were on the road again. Another glorious day. In the bright sun, the sea was glittering, way below us. I had given Henry a few pages to read about her so that he would be able to refresh his memory, because he said he remembered years ago reading some of her short stories. She was such a passionate woman and a brilliant writer, but lived such a tragic life. It is hard to believe that things went so wrong for her. I felt excited and hoped Henry would find the day interesting. Maybe I was imagining it, but I thought if I could involve him with my project, it might help him over his grief.

After reading her letters to John Middleton Murry written from the south of France, and knowing what a romantic writer she was, her descriptions of the town of Bandol and of Menton, were so vivid, I wanted to see where she lived and worked. Virginia Woolf had written that she was jealous of her work, and because of this she didn't read her, even though they had been friends.

The notes I gave Henry, as well as her letters were part of my research., She was a New Zealand writer born in 1888 who died in 1920 at the age of 32. In 1905 she went to England to study the cello, but when she gave up trying to become a musician after her arrival in London, she began writing short stories, which still survive today. She became a member of the Bloomsbury Group making friends with Virginia Woolf, Lady Ottoline Morrell, Bertrand Russell, D.H. Lawrence and many of the writers of that period. She fell in love with the writer, John Middleton Murry and they lived together in London.

However Katherine developed tuberculosis and her doctor advised her to spend the winters in a warmer climate. He suggested Morocco or further south, but said if that was impossible, then the south of France would do. She decided on Bandol, then Menton, which was an unfortunate choice because it was one of the worst places she could go to cure the disease because of the damp atmosphere.

I thought that to see where she had lived in Menton, and to follow in her footsteps through the palm trees and the pine woods would be tremendously romantic, and possibly inspire me..Her letters were full of wonderful descriptions of her daily walks.

Being from New Zealand she was in constant fear that she would have to return there if things didn't work out in Europe. Already she had gone back there once and was very unhappy and restless and begged her father to let her return which he did, giving her a small living allowance to live on.

After she had been diagnosed with T.B. she risked her relationship with John Middleton Murry leaving him to try to recover from her illness by following the sun and staying in the south of France. During her stay there, she not only wrote short stories but began a long correspondence with Murry who could not, or would not leave England, except for one visit to see her. In 1915 she wrote to him from Menton. "This place is so full of our love that every little walk I take is a passionate pilgrimage."

She had two disastrous marriages, one of which only lasted one day, her adolescent bisexuality, her illness, her love affairs, her quick wit likens her to someone like Dorothy Parker, especially as she became famous for her brilliant short stories. She had a passionate friendship with D.H. Lawrence and he compared her to Dickens and later wrote that he used her as the model for Gudrun in 'Women in Love."

Her biographer, Antony Alpers was assisted by material freely given by both her husbands and a close friend whom she called "wife." Also by her two sisters, a cousin, and two former lovers.

Her husband Middleton Murry left Alpers entirely free to publish whatever he had discovered that was true.

When she first arrived in the south of France, in 1915 she was suffering from tuberculosis when she finally left in 1921 she was dying. What lay between were four flights from English winters, four futile pilgrimages to the sun. It was Menton that killed her. Menton with its still, enervating, pine-laden climate, fatal for consumptives. I have no where seen so many gravestones to the young – among them Aubrey Beardsley's dead at twenty-six – as in Menton's cemetery.

She had gone first to Bandol. This was a beach resort where some of the first tourists were Thomas Mann, Aldous Huxley, Marcel Pagnol and Mistinguett had stayed, but she found it too commercial so moved further along the coast to Menton on the other side of Nice.

John Middleton Murry came to visit her and they went for walks among the hills behind the town, however he soon returned to London leaving her to recuperate for the winter months.

She wrote every day, sometimes twice a day to him and one wonders if he answered as frequently. She was bored no doubt, even though she was beginning to fall in love with the beauty of the south of France and she describes many of her days vividly as she went on numerous walks, missing him constantly.

"Ah, I wanted you today. Today I have longed for you. Have you known that? Can I long for you and you not know?"

December 20th

"A lovely 'gold dust' day. From early morning the fishermen have been passing and the little boats with red sails put out at dawn. When I woke this morning and opened the shutters and saw the dimpling sea I knew I was beginning to love this place—this south of France. Yesterday I went for a walk. The palm trees after the rain were magnificent, so firm and so green and standing up like stiff bouquets before the Lord."

"Oh, Bogey, it is the most heavenly day. Every little tree feels it and waves faintly from delight. The femme de chambre called to the gardener just now as she beat the next door mattress out of the window – "Fait bon?" and he said "Ah, delicieux!" which seemed to me very funny for a gardener."

Her letters to Murray described her infatuation for the scenery and her daily life in the south of France. Her poetry, her short stories were all about the region.

At that time, she was not married to John, so she was looking forward to a wedding when she returned to England. Most of her letters to him were love letters, looking forward to the day when they would wed. She wrote to him. " I wish you could see the winds playing on the dark blue sea today, the clouds are like swans,the air tastes like fruit. Yesterday I went for a long scrambling walk in the woods, on the other side of the railway. There are no roads there, just a little track and old mule paths. Parts are quite wild and overgrown, then in all sorts of unexpected faery places you find a little clearing- the ground cultivated in tiny red terraces and sheltered by olive trees. There grow the jonquils, daffodils, new green peas and big abundant rose bushes, they are dream places. Every now and then I would hear a rustle in the bushes and an old, old, woman her head tied up in a black kerchief, would come creeping through the thick tangle with a bunch of that pink heath across her shoulders. Once I found myself right at the very top of a hill and below there lay an immense valley - surrounded by mountains - very high ones- and it was so clear you could see every pointed pine, every little zig-zag track - the black stems of the olives showing sooty and soft among the silvery green."

"Oh Bogey, how I longed for my playfellow! Why weren't you with me?" (I wondered if Bogarde had ever been called Bogey, a strange coincidence, if so)

And, another letter written on Christmas Eve. "Yesterday after I had posted your letter I went to the Market. You know where that is, in front of that curious little Church. Yesterday the Market was full of roses, branches of mandarins and flowers of all kinds. There was also a little old man selling blue spectacles and rings 'contre la rhumatisme' and a funny fat old woman waddling about."

That day Henry and I found that old market, but found the house closed and boarded up.Her letters describe her joy at being there and her love affair with the area.

As we drove though the town I kept talking on.

"Even though she was incredibly lonely, and in pain, she wrote every day. Mainly letters to John, but also to friends. The atmosphere of the area enchanted her. She read a great deal and said to alleviate her insomnia and night fevers, she would read Dickens, but that sometimes even he did not calm her."

She wrote, "I don't dare to work any more tonight. I suffer so frightfully from insomnia here and from night terrors. My work excites me so tremendously that I almost feel insane at night and I have been at it with hardly a break all day. But there is a great black bird flying over me, and I am so frightened he'll settle - so terrified I don't know exactly what kind he is. If I were not working here, with war and anxiety I should go mad, I think."

March 4th

"Yesterday we went to La Turbie. It's up, up, high, high on the tops of the mountains. I could hardly bear it yesterday. I was so much in love with you. I kept seeing it all, for you – wishing for you – longing for you. The rosemary is in flower (our plant is). The almond trees, pink and white, there are wild cherry trees and prickly pear white among the olives. Apple trees are just in their first rose and white – wild hyacinths and violets are tumbled out of Flora's wicker ark and are everywhere. And over everything, like a light, are the lemon and orange trees glowing .If I saw one house which was ours, I saw twenty. I know we shall never live in such houses, but still they are ours - little houses with terraces and a verandah – with bean fields in bloom with a bright scatter of anemones all over the gardens. When we reached the mountain tops we got out and lay on the grass, looking down, down - into the valleys and over Monaco.

"We stayed there about 2 hours and then dropped down by another road to Monte – the light and the shadow were divided on the hills, but the sun was still in the air, all the time – the sea was very rosy with a pale big moon over by Bordighera. We got home by 6.30 and there was my fire, the bed turned down – hot milk - May waiting to take off all my things. Did you enjoy it, Madam?

Henry and I became almost inseparable. He wanted company, and I suppose I did too. We were both going through emotional turmoil and we were both trying to help each other. Curiously neither of us had any physical chemistry for each other, so except for a friendly type of kiss goodnight at the end of an evening, that was it. We needed companionship and neither of us wanted to rock the boat.

I told him about my acting career, and losing my first love, Michael by being away from him so long. How I knew it could easily happen again. It is all part of the acting business. It's inescapable.

One night we went to Ragtime, which was a nightclub near the new Palais. They had a quartet who played ragtime and 1920's music. Back to the Jazz Age at last! It was a great place to hear a local pianist who was exceptionally good, and a man, a stranger, sent us over a bottle of Champagne. We didn't know why. We nodded our thanks as the waiter opened the bottle for us.

"I am so curious," I said to Henry, "why don't we ask him over and see why he gave us the champagne?" He agreed as he was just as mystified as I was. We beckoned him over and he sat with us. He then proceeded to tell us the story of his life, he just wanted to talk to us, another lonely guy I thought. How many were there?

Each day I would try to entertain Henry until he was over his worst pain. I realized that some one would take my place soon enough if I left, because he needed so badly to talk to someone. So what if I stayed on here. We could go on like this for years. I could join the local library, play tennis, sit in the sun. I was an actress of a certain age, with no work back in England, I bet many women of my age would find him attractive and could make a good life for themselves out here. It is the Riviera after all. I couldn't imagine living through another winter in England, so here was my chance.

One day when we were driving along the small road on Cap Antibes, I suddenly had an idea.

"I really would love to see inside some of these fabulous homes. They all look so beautiful, the gardens are exquisite, how can we get inside some of them? There has to be a way."

I too had been writing articles for magazine back home, so I thought that they might be interested in an article about British and American women who live in the Riviera. Some of them would have very interesting stories I thought. Perhaps I would contact some of them, and we could go and interview them in their houses. Henry was keen, and said he could bring his camera and we could say that he was my cameraman. I looked up in the pages of the Nice Martin to find some of these women pictured at local society events. Perhaps there would be some writers among them.

Chapter Five

How much fun we had after we had contacted these people. I found out that there was a British cabaret singer living in Cap D'Antibes who used to be the rage in London and her risque songs were the talk of the town. She was in her late 80's when we met her, and still writing songs and working on a cantata. Her whole life had been devoted to music and composing. She was an inspiration as she was so full of energy and creative spirit. I wondered if I would still have her kind of energy at the same age. I believe it is a God given gift, you either have it or you don't. Next we called on an American lady who lived in a fabulous house right on the water's edge, almost next door to the house where David Niven lived. Her main passion was fashion. She followed Yves St. Laurent each season, making sure she was at each showing in Paris. I found it rather difficult to imagine why she was living down here, away from the big city. Several other characters, we interviewed had all found a life for themselves which was far different from wherever they had come from, originally.

One night, I had been to a movie at the local cinema. I was on my own so I decided while walking back along the Croisette to have a nightcap at the Carlton. It was a full moon that night, so the view was memorable. As I sat there, a group of people came to sit nearby, destroying whatever peace there was, and they took up three tables between them. They were speaking English and by their conversation I discovered that they had been to the same movie. Evidently a friend of one made it, and they all knew him and the director, so a celebration was taking place. After a few minutes I decided to leave because it was late and the ambience had been shattered. One of the men came over to me, he had been drinking quite a lot, but wanted to talk. He was quite good looking and was curious about me. He looked a little bit like Hugh Grant, very tall, distinguished looking in a way, with a lock of black hair falling across his face, and a nice smile.

"Do you mind?" he said, as he sat down beside me.

"I don't have much choice do I?"

"What are doing here all alone?"

I detected an accent, not British.

As if he knew what I was thinking. "We are here seeing my friend's movie."

"Most of us are from Canada. I used to be, but I live here now."

"That must be great." I wished he would leave.

"I'm John" he said "John Garston" He leant forward to shake my hand. He was wearing a blue blazer and blue shirt, probably from Brook Brothers, not bad, he seemed rather civilized.

"I'm Nicole" I deliberately didn't say my last name, in case it rang a bell.

The waiter came and picked up the little black folder with my signature on the bill.

It was time to leave.

John finished his drink, called over to the others and waved goodbye.

"I have to leave because I have to find my car, I've forgotten where I parked it."

I got up and walked down the steps with him. I think he must have found me attractive, because he suddenly invited me to go to the Casino with him. I hadn't been inside the Palm Beach casino and every time I passed it I was curious to see inside. It was very late, and I said thanks, but no thanks. And continued on my way. When I got home, I suddenly thought what a lost opportunity. I could have had a good look inside the world-renowned place, and I felt stupid that I hadn't taken up his offer, especially as this is the time of night that the place comes alive. Usually way past my usual bedtime. I dimly remembered that women are not allowed in the Casino unescorted. So I had missed my chance, as I knew Henry wouldn't go there. Not that we had ever talked about it. Was I getting old? Was I becoming set in my ways? An exciting invitation, to see play in action and see the décor of the place. I suddenly decided that I did want to go after all. I was wide awake now, and kicking myself.

Here was the opportunity to meet new people, all kinds of people. It was an international scene after all. Isn't that what I wanted? A few minutes later, minutes feeling full of irritation, I phoned the Casino, and had him paged. When he came to the phone I explained that I really would like to meet him there. He told me where to enter, which door, because there were several it seemed and to find him at the Roulette table.

I wasn't disappointed I had changed my mind. He reminded me to take my passport and surrender it at the front door before I was allowed to be escorted to his table. He had left my name with instructions. The scene was something like out of a James Bond movie. Gambling tables, under green shaded lamps, red plush curtains, ladies in jewels, much activity and such interesting looking characters. From then on it was an unforgettable evening. John insisted I have champagne, and insisted on giving me some 'play' money to play some Roulette, which I did. I was determined to give him my winnings but there weren't any actually. He was in such a good mood, I didn't realize at the time that he was in one of his manic moods, and he said how pleased he was to be paged in the Casino,a rare occurrence and one which carried prestige evidently. "It's very impressive to be paged at the bar!" He seemed extraordinarily happy. The place was jumping. Time was forgotten in such an exciting and colorful place.

I was very surprised to see that finally when we walked through the front door that faces the Mediterranean, dawn was actually breaking across the sky. We found his car, a sports car with the roof still down, and he said.

"Come on, I'm going to show you the real Riviera."

What the hell, why not? I knew if I was kidnapped or disappeared that Henry would report it. Even so, I wondered if he would give me a day or two before he did so.

We drove up north behind Cannes, on to the top Corniche, and then through Grasse, up further through the villages, which dotted the mountain side.

Suddenly I realized that I had been up all night, but didn't feel tired at all. The way he was driving the convertible, around the bends and though the villages at high speed, kept one awake. Swifts, dozens of them together, swooped down in front of the car, they were everywhere. We arrived in Cabris..a legendary village, just as the sun was climbing up in the sky. The view was sensational, looking down the valley out towards the sea, now in the background. This is the village where the "Little Prince" was written…and home to the author. We drove on further and around another few bends, down a country lane, to where he had just bought a house. We drove up the driveway, and there was an old stone mas, beautifully located on the side of the hill. It was being renovated and workmen were already working on the top part of the house. They were also building a swimming pool in front of the house. Much later, when I went there again, everything was finished.

I admired him for taking the leap and leaving his homeland to try and set up house down here. His French was very good, but these men were Italian, and he didn't know too much of the language, so he was probably being ripped off by all these workers. Foreigners always seem to be if they don't really speak the language. Reading about the nightmares that the author Frances Mayes went through when she wrote about her experiences in "Under the Tuscan Sky." It didn't help matters when his mother kept writing from Ottawa, to "take life seriously and come back and settle down." He was too determined, and he managed to get quite a good job the next year with the Cannes Festival administration.

I tried to sleep in a tiny back bedroom while he went on working with the men around the house. There was quite a lot of noise so sleep was nearly impossible, Around lunchtime, we drove back up the hill and had a wonderful lunch at the old restaurant in the village. It was when I had a glass of wine that the tiredness really sank in. After lunch I did manage to sleep, and later that afternoon, when the workmen had gone, he drove me back down into Cannes. It had been a wonderful journey and he introduced me to some British people we met in the local garage who also had bought a house in Frejas, another village near by. There was a large group of British up there, living happily in the mountains. A few days later he phoned and we decided to meet again the following weekend. He wanted to show me a few places for rent.

"Or you could buy something." He laughed

"It's too early for that. Maybe I could rent for awhile."

It seemed quite a coincidence that I had met such an adventurous guy, who obviously loved living down here and helped me get to know the area.

Chapter Six

Next day, I decided to check out the tennis at the Majestic Courts behind the hotel. I had no partner but I thought that there would be a pro around who could help. The Club had a Pro who had his own office and there was a Clubroom with a little bar, three women in white were sitting there. They told me that there was a ladies round robin every morning and I would be welcome to join them. I bought some tennis clothes then and there, and there was a second hand racket for sale as well. So I was all set

Earlier, I had received another e mail from Nigel, who was now asking for my phone number. No way. I was determined not to let him persuade me to return. I was angry and annoyed with him and told him not to write again, as I would not be replying. Period.

This time I meant it and wished I'd never written in the first place. From them on I just deleted every thing that came from him.

I was pleased to meet a woman named Pauline at the courts. She is a short slim brunette who reminded me a little of Diane Keaton. She has a bubbly personality, an American with no nonsense manner and plays tennis very well. We hit it off immediately. After the game, we had a cool drink and she told me about her life. Her house was in view of the tennis court, so she only had a short walk each day.

We became friends. She invited me to her house for tea. It was a lovely house with a nice garden that she loved to tend herself.

"It keeps me busy."

The house was full of treasure. She had old china plates on the wall, in the Dragon pattern that my mother used to own. The floors were wood, parquet with oriental rugs in each room. Her dining room had a Chippendale set of chairs and I knew that they must be worth a fortune these days. She lived alone, but obviously entertained a great deal. I guessed that she must have had a lover as she didn't have a husband.

Divorced ten years ago, she knew what I was thinking.

"Actually I have to thank a chap called George for all this." She laughed

"What do you mean?"

"Well I was living in New Jersey and I was very unhappy. My husband was a workaholic and I was so bored I left and went to live in New York. I got a job and commuted each weekend. I met a fabulous man; we had an affair for two years. I adored him, he was everything to me, I was blissfully happy. He was married, but I thought he would divorce his wife eventually and marry me. How naïve can you be. One day he took me out to lunch and said it was over, that he had met someone else, and that he didn't love me any more. This all sounds so cliché and it is, and I never thought it would happen to me."

I listened because she was so calm about it even though it must have been so painful to tell me.

"I thought of suicide. He was my whole life, I didn't know what I was going to do. He just made all the difference in my life. I couldn't work, I couldn't sleep. I gave up my job and moved back to New Jersey because Manhattan was full of reminders, every place every restaurant where we had gone, haunted me. I bumped into him in a video store one day and he cut me. I couldn't have that happen again. But you know what? I now thank him for dumping me, because after I had recovered from the devastation, it made me, forced me to change my life. I had to end my marriage, I couldn't stay in New Jersey, and so I decided to come to France. I love it here. I love the atmosphere."

She smiled and leaned forward to pour some more tea in my cup.

Suddenly the thought occurred to me that I had Nigel to thank for me coming here. If we hadn't had such a row I wouldn't be here on the Riviera. I suppose the only saying is true...if you are given lemons, make lemonade.

Pauline had realized that George had unknowingly given her a new life.

"You must meet my close friend, Julia. She has almost the exact story, however it's even better because in her new life, like phoenix rising from the ashes of a disastrous affair, she has become a very successful and famous artist."

"Not Julia Gearheart?"

"Yes, that's the one."

"I saw her work here at the Carlton."

"She always has her exhibitions there, before they go to Paris."

"How do you know her?"

"Heavens I can't remember I've known her for so long."

"I'd love to meet her."

"She also, believe it or not, is divorced and their stories are almost the same. Desperation drove her over here; she had a terrible time at first. She like me knew that suicide was not an option, but something really different had to be done. She had no money, which made it more difficult. She got herself a nanny job, looking after an American family in Paris and then took classes at an Art School there." Pauline explained. "You must meet her."

I told her I was writing a book about the writers down her who had retraced the writers of the 1920's.

'How terrific! What a great idea. Trouble is I don't read much, tennis is my life!" she laughed. I envied women who could make playing sport their passion. Playing golf or croquet or tennis, perhaps I should try it. Forget this writing business. However now, I had someone to read my first drafts, besides Henry.

True to his word, John called. He had lined up some apartments for me to see. When he picked me up in the car, I could see he wasn't in a very good mood. Little did I know this was part of his manic behaviour and I wish I had known about it then. One day ecstatically happy, the next moody and irritable. The afternoon didn't go well. First of all there was a cold breeze blowing, not the mistral he said, and then he had picked places really difficult to find. We drove into Antibes, and found two small flats there, in the old town. One had a great view of the harbour, but is was very small, and seemed rather damp. The other one was down an old stone alleyway, and all the noises from the adjoining apartments came through the window. The kitchen was awful, and it turned me off house hunting completely.

John muttered that I didn't know what I wanted, but then again, he had given me no choice. We drove back to Cannes in silence. I felt unhappy that we had had a lovely time the week before, so made my excuses and said that maybe we could meet again in a few weeks. We didn't. I knew he was always there if I needed advice. He was in such a bad mood that I decided that it would be difficult to keep a relationship going with him because you would never know what kind of mood he'd be in. Forming new friendships is hard enough without dealing with someone who had mental problems.

Next day Henry was around very early with the car because we had decided to drive over to see Somerset Maugham's villa on Cap St.Jean Ferrat. The coast road gets very busy after eleven o'clock so we wanted to drive there without the traffic. We knew the villa was rented now, so it would not be possible to go through the house, however we wanted to see the view. The same view that Maugham wrote so eloquently about. We were not disappointed. We parked the car off the road and walked around the property. There was a red clay tennis court, in among the trees, and I knew that Maugham's house guests had played there. I thought of my favourite nostalgic imagination moment….how I would have liked to have been around that court when Maugham, Coward and several others were playing, then up to the house for a quick swim and lunch.. I imagined they gossiped and said witty but cruel things about all kinds of people. Both Maugham and Coward were great imitators so they probably acted out many situations and dialogue over meals. Maugham's house was fabulously furnished, and he had a great art collection..

Ah, but those days were gone. Now, we live in the present. Somewhere there are famous writers, living and working down here, now, living the experiences day by day that future biographers will write about. I wonder where they are? Why do I live in the past? Why care about these long dead writers, what's the point? The landscape down here is exquisite and it is very difficult to understand if there is any real emotional regret, in people such as Gore Vidal, when they go back to live in the U.S. or England.

We drove on to the Grand Hotel Du Cap -Ferrat, just down the road from the villa. The hotel had just been renovated and was now a super luxury hotel. I felt sad that when these hotels decide to renovate, they can't help destroying some of the magic of the past, especially if they throw out the existing furniture and china, paintings and carpets. I like to think that I am walking on the carpet that Maugham walked on, that he sat at the bar in the same bar stool that sits there now. If they have to redecorate or replace the worn furniture, I wonder why they don't just replicate the original, perhaps the wicker chairs, or the leather banquettes, it should be easy enough to replace such things. Not some new white upholstered sofa with tassells and glitz. Somehow seeing the photos of him and all his friends, drinking in the bar, didn't have the desired effect of nostalgia. It was all too modern now and all the old furniture had gone. But the building was still there, and the view. Now we had to find some other way of recapturing the nostalgia.

"John took me house hunting yesterday." I mentioned in the car.

"How did you go, or rather where did you go?"

"Along this road, actually. We saw two places in Antibes."

"Well we will be there in five minutes. Shall we stop for lunch?"he suggested.

We went to Chez Felix, a place I had wanted to visit as it is known as Graham Greene's favourite restaurant, and we had been told that it had not been changed. The menu was still the same, Henry observed, and he said that the clientele hadn't changed either. There was still that incredible frisson, the aroma of a thousand dishes cooked here, conversations held, wine drunk, the atmosphere was full of the magic of the past. We ordered the lamb which was pink and tender, creamy gravy which was delicious with crisp baked potatoes, tiny green peas, together with a bottle of the local vin rose. The wine of Provence. We compared thoughts about Greene and his various works and we came to the conclusion that he was a tortured man who used his writing to try to exorcise his demons. It seems that most Catholic writers who have a background of Christian faith have lots to feel guilty about, because of their childhood indoctrination.

"He certainly went overboard, in the other direction entirely."

"You've read a lot of him then?" I asked.

"A long time ago. Then of course I read his autobiography and found out about his personal life. Not that brilliant. He must have been a very complex man to be able to live with himself, that's all I can say."

I wondered naively I suppose, if when you become a famous writer, and people write you celebratory letters, does that mean you can live any kind of life you want?

"People in the theatre take pains not to go over the top."

"Everyone I guess except John Gielgud. It is astonishing how little his personal behaviour affected his career."

After lunch we went to sit in the Town Square and watch the world go by. I was tired of driving as we had been doing all morning. How beautiful the day was, I knew that it would be wonderful to be able to stay here and work.

It was interesting that Henry had read a great deal about the writers who had lived down here. We had passed the famous beach which many writers had discovered.

I read an extract from the British writer, Cyril Connolly's novel 'Rock Pool' that I had brought with me......

"It was his favourite beach: for him the white sand, the pale translucent water, the cicadas' jigging away at their perpetual rumba, the smell of rosemary and cactus, the corrugations of sunshine on the bright Aleppo pines, held the whole classic essence of the Mediterranean."

Driving back to Cannes, we were both silent.

"What are you thinking about" said Henry.

"Just wondering about friends back home. I sometimes miss them. I have no real family left, but I do have some close friends. How about you?"

It was the first tine he had really opened up about his life before Cannes. He obviously didn't want to talk about it very much because I think it reminded him of his marriage and working life, so far in the past now.

"My parents were living nearby for years. Both of them ended up in a nursing home and they died within months of each other. I was an only child, so it was hard taking care of them. They didn't ask for much, except company and so we were really tied to the spot, so to speak. Couldn't travel too much. But we did manage to get down here once in a while for a few days, That's when we decided that we wanted to retire here."

He asked me about my family.

"Both my parents are dead, so I really had no relatives left. Part of the family, my grandmother's family emigrated to Australia early in the 1900's. My parents used to keep in touch with them, mostly at Christmas and birthdays."

"Are they still there?"

"I don't really know we lost touch. A great aunt of mine used to write to me when I was in drama school in London, encouraging me. She was an elocution teacher, and wanted to know how I was doing. She came to London once to see me in a play, and we had so much to talk about. I really loved her for her support and enthusiasm"

Thinking of her I realized she would love to hear about what I'm doing. I decided to write her a letter even though I didn't know if she was still living.

Driving back I knew I had to break the back of my project. I had to start writing soon. It was time.

We had been to practically every Museum. We had seen where Picasso worked, had seen the Chagall masterpieces and Museums, up down and across the Alps Maritime and I had lots to remember. Dennis said that we could share the car. I could use it anytime I needed it which was a great help getting around.

So that was it, as I drove down the hill into Cannes. Little did I know how hard it was going to be. I kept going over the terrible row I had with Nigel, and lying in bed at night, it all played back like an old film. I had tried to make a friend of his son that just made their relationship even worse.

Next day I started. First the walk along the beach. If you get up early enough, you don't see anyone, only the workmen sweeping the beach, getting ready to put the rows of deck chairs and umbrellas out for the masses who will come to lie in the sun much later. I loved the early mornings. Nowhere can you find such peace as on a beach, perhaps a forest or a mountain top but the water creates such calm. The beauty of the place, somewhere.

The first day went slowly. I had not set myself a number of words to write each day as I thought that would be too terrifying. so boring. How many people really want to know? I asked myself. Good question. Why do we all think that we can create?

I smiled at the thought of all the women, across the world, right at this minute, sitting down trying to write a book. Millions maybe. Or others painting a picture, practising the piano, learning their scales, singers, actors all struggling in this fugitive art. It boggles the mind that there are so many of us. I wished I had been born with a different set of genes. No creative ones, just the facts. Again Dirk surfaced with a funny line from his autobiography, something along the lines that go like this " All those women up in Hampstead typing away. They write a few chapters, then do a quick whip around with the vacuum cleaner and call themselves writers."

Writers and actors all have the constant pressure of what they will working on next.

One young actress once asked Somerset Maugham for advice only to receive the answer, "Forget about acting, go and marry a rich American instead". How cynical. Maybe he was writing the Razor's Edge at the time.

Each day, first, the walk. If it was raining, it was difficult to catch that energy you get from walking. I did exercises instead. Boring. But it helped to get started. I took the phone off the hook, it is so easy to be distracted. Any excuse. Sharpening pencils is good. Eating an orange is good. I suppose if I had a garden, I might have started gardening. Digging a ditch was easy to staring at a blank piece of paper or screen. Writer's block and I'd only just started. It was easy to think about other things. Like what will I have for dinner tonight, or maybe I should cook for Henry tonight. Should I go to the market before it closes. Stop it. I knew I would weaken. Discipline was needed. Thank God I'd given up smoking.

One day shortly after I had finished the first chapter, during the afternoon, when I had put the phone back on. Pauline called to invite me to meet her friend Julie. I was really looking forward to meeting her.

Chapter Seven

I walked over to Pauline's house and up through her garden, ringing the front door, I didn't know what Julia would be like. As usual Pauline was dressed in well fitting slacks and top, looking fresh and cool, with little gold earrings and bracelet. We walked out to the patio at the back. Julia got up. She was a lovely blonde woman. Attractive and friendly. Her hair was piled up in a bun and a touch of pink lipstick, a simple blue dress and sandals. We sat and talked for at least an hour. She wanted to know what I had been doing and I found out about her life. I was totally overwhelmed by her business like and professional attitude. She was obviously a very serious artist and had her plans for the rest of the year all mapped out. She lived here and had a studio here, but she went to Italy to have her bronzes cast and to do the primary work on her casting. She was sketching as we talked, and she had done some lovely sketches of figures. That was her specialty. Figures, almost all of them in motion, carrying a child up in the air, or two figures, reaching out to each other. Almost like ballet figures. They were very lyrical and beautiful. I suddenly felt very lazy and uncreative. Here was a powerhouse of creative energy and almost a passion to keep working.

Her story was fascinating. Originally from Canada she won a grant to go to study in Italy. She had to work. During her studies, she had the idea of writing to every mayor in towns near by, and offering to do a bust for them in bronze. Many of them said yes, they would be delighted. She managed to do some very influential men and then some Art Gallery in that town or city would exhibit these busts and that way she gained exposure, sales, and commissions. The Art Magazines started noticing her work, and she was awarded another grant and won some awards, which brought in money.. She gave me a brochure which showed her work so far, some of which had been bought by Museums back in Canada.

I walked back home realizing just how much her whole life was devoted to working, and just how many of us just fritter our lives away doing nothing.

Above all, I envied her passion, her drive, her desire for fame, or rather perhaps recognition, and her dedication. It seemed to come to her so easily. Sitting there watching her work, drawing the figures that she would later turn into bronze sculptures purchased by museums, parks and palatial homes. . Her work was astonishing and she obviously has great talent. I hoped that we could meet again but I knew she would not have much free time.

Phoning Pauline as soon as I got back, I thanked her for the meeting. She didn't seem to feel any of the thoughts I was having.

"What are we doing with our lives?" I said.

"What do you mean?"

"Well look at Julia. I feel so earthbound after meeting her. She is so productive and creative. And so professional too."

She laughed and I knew then that she didn't feel the same emotion.

"I knew you would like her. She has achieved so much. Like you."

"No, nothing like me. I haven't achieved anything like she has. She has practically achieved immortality. Those sculptures will be around this earth, much longer than we will."

She laughed again and I knew I couldn't express any further thoughts to her. I would just have to work things out for myself.

A few weeks later after meeting Julia for a drink several times, an idea began to form in my head. I was still working on my book, writing even just a little every day, and slowly re-writing when I couldn't get anything new down on paper. Julia was leaving to go to her foundry in Italy, to do the casting for several pieces of work. I wanted to go with her and watch the whole process. She couldn't afford to do all the pieces in bronze but it would be a wonderful experience to see her work, and to be part of what seems to be an artist's colony at Pietra Santa in Italy. She stayed at a hotel in Forte dei Marmi, a beach resort close by.

The next day I asked Julia if I could join her there for a week or so. She usually hired a car and often drove into Florence. She had to go to Paris first and then was flying down to Pisa and then on to Pietra Santa in a week or two. She could meet me there, if I could get to Pisa, then we could drive down together.

Meanwhile, I resolved to do as much writing as possible before leaving so if I missed a day or two there, it wouldn't be so bad. When I told Henry of my plan he thought the break would do me good, and he was all for it.

"I will miss you of course, but it really does sound as if it would be an interesting experience." He was still undecided what to do about his life and was struggling to set up a daily routine for himself that would keep him busy.

Pauline was amused but pleased I had decided to go.

"If you don't speak Italian, you may find it difficult" was all she had to say.

How right she was. After meeting Julia at the airport in Pisa, we drove in her rented car to the hotel. It was truly a lovely place. The hotel was a small pastoral place with lovely gardens and a swimming pool on the lawn. However it was a shock to discover that no one spoke English or French. Not a word and I had to rely on Julia to get me a room.

She didn't know what I would pay but just booked the room. When I went back to the desk later to ask, in case it was above my budget, I couldn't understand a word, even when they wrote it down. Was that 100 dollars a day or a 1000! Then came the dining room that night and the menu! The menu was hand written in purple ink and you'd think that some of the names of dishes would be familiar, but none of them were. The scrawl was incomprehensible. Nothing looked familiar.

Julia was tired after a day of driving and was impatient with me.

"Just order what I'm having" she muttered. She then ordered for me.

Thank goodness she didn't order calamari, or some shell fish which I'm allergic to.

In the morning, she was in much better spirits. We drove up to the foundry. What a magical place it was. Five or six people came up to say hullo, after she had parked the car. She comes here every year, so they know her. Here I was suddenly in the center of an art studio, right in the midst of all these people who were busy creating original work. It was very exciting. A whole other world.

There were two American sculptors there, so I could speak English to them, thank goodness. In fact they really made the whole trip for me as I was totally lost not speaking Italian. One German man, spoke English well, and he took me over to show off his latest work, a larger than life, almost twelve feet of a bronze Atlas, with the Globe on his shoulders.

It was magnificent. Standing in a shed near by. The company who had commissioned it, a Bank, had gone out of business and he had only received a down payment for the work, so he was badly in debt to the foundry and had to find a buyer as soon as possible. It was finished and ready to be shipped when he found out about the bank.

“Do you know anyone who would like him?”

"I wish I did.” Let me think about it.

It needed to be in the foyer or lobby of a Bank somewhere. Maybe a hotel? I doubted that my bank in Cannes would be interested. I took several photos and one of him standing beside the work, to show the actual size of it, just in case I had a brainwave, I could easily see it standing in a magnificent lobby somewhere in Manhattan, if only I'd known someone there.

He said he would sell it for a thousand dollars, which is what the bronze alone had cost him.

“I will try and ask a few people. It really is a masterpiece.”

“It took me over six months, and I let other commissions go, because of it.”

He was very grateful for my interest as he was obviously extremely upset, not only by the financial loss but every thing else. He was hurting badly.

“Would you have dinner with me tonight? I know a place down by the beach.”

The hotel was in Forte dei Marmi, so were lots of little places there. I didn't relish the idea that if I dined with Julia again I would have to have what Julia had at the hotel, because she couldn't be bothered to translate the menu for me. However she may have expected me to eat with her at the hotel. After all I had come with her. I went over and asked her.

"Please do." She said, "I am going to be exhausted after today. I may not even eat when I get back. I am going to Florence tomorrow to get more materials. If you would like to come with me, let's meet in the lobby at 10 am."

"That's great. Yes, I'd love to." I knew she didn't want me to stay and watch her work. So I suggested I leave them, and come back for her later.

That evening, I was ready when George picked me up in his car. He had shaved and changed which made him look very different. No longer in his work clothes, he was a huge man seemed almost as big as his sculpture.

We ate in a small quiet restaurant near the beach.

"They specialize in cannelloni here. All kinds, I like the lobster best."

"Anything with pesto sauce please."

"Oh you like pesto…then you should have the pesto lasagne with the melon and ham to start. I think a bottle of red, don't you?"

The waiter had already placed cheese and pate with bread on the table.

The meal was delicious and we ended with the best ice cream I've ever tasted. Home made of course. We were off the tourist track, and I loved the feeling of being in a traditional old Italian place, where they all seemed to know each other.

After dinner, we walked with most of the residents of the town, along the long boardwalk at the back of the sandy beach. It was a lovely evening, the stars were glittering and appeared so very near. I looked at all the local couples, and their relatives, all walking along greeting each other. So this was what everyone did after a day of work. It was lovely to be there. It must have been like this for centuries. It was magical.

George was full of his sorrows, and I had to keep changing the subject because he kept talking about the bastards who had let him down. I could imagine how bitter he must have felt, but I also wondered how long it would take him to find a buyer for his Atlas.

When we got back to the hotel, he seemed to want an invitation to come up to my room, but it was easier enough to excuse myself, saying that we were making an early start to Florence in the morning. As if 10 am was early, but I didn't tell him the departure time.

He wandered off, and my heart went out to him. I hoped that he would work again on something else, although he was very discouraged.

Julia and I drove into Florence, the next day. I had been there before and had seen all the tourists spots, so I wanted to be with Julia and go to the places where she got her materials. Huge galleries and warehouses, with plaster and finished busts, bodies, figures everywhere. I remember a scene from a Zeffirelli's film "Tea with Mussolini" showing one of these wonderful places. How magnificent they were. Whole rows of marble and plaster busts and full sized statues. It made me want to buy them all.

Driving back to Forte dei Marmi the scenery was spectacular. Lovely vistas of the mountains and at that time of day, they were all in various shades of purple. A wonderful glaze of purple and mist. I made up my mind I would do a painting when I got back to Cannes. This was a different light, but just as beautiful.

The next few days were fascinating watching these sculptors work. I learnt the technique of how they worked in plaster, marble and bronze. The marble of course, came from the nearby famous quarries. Michelangelo had used the same marble.

During the next week, I saw George every night. Julia didn't mind as she was always so exhausted and didn't want to go for a promenade after working all day, which involved mostly standing up. He started to become a pest. I insisted on paying my way for drinks and dinner after the first evening, but he began to embarrass me with his romantic talk and his obvious frustrations of all kinds. I had seen what I had come to see, I had soaked up the atmosphere, which was inspiring, so it was time to leave. I took the cowardly way out, and told George one morning at the foundry that I would be leaving that afternoon.

We exchanged addresses and phone numbers but we both doubted if we would see each other again. I hadn't invited him down to Cannes and he was going back to Germany, where instinct told me, he had a wife, although I never asked.

I took the train back to Cannes. Next day, I went out and bought paints, brushes and canvasses. I had promised I would do that painting of the mountains outside Florence. Besides I wanted something else to do besides sitting writing all day. I needed to diversify.

Painting was a way to cope with the difficulty of writing

Chapter Eight

A week later, a surprise came in the form of a letter, which had been forwarded on by my agent, from a solicitor in London. It seems that my Australian great aunt had died recently, and in her will she had stated that she was leaving a little cottage for me, which was, believe it or not, somewhere outside Cannes. As I had told Henry just the other day, we had lost touch years ago. What a wonderful surprise. I really couldn't believe it. It must be fate, or something. I knew I was a favorite of hers and immediately felt guilty I hadn't kept in touch.. But that was ages ago.

I hadn't seen or heard of her for years. I knew she used to come to France when there were school holidays, and she had her yearly break, but no idea she had a cottage here..

I phoned Henry.

"Henry, guess what! I have some terrific news! I've just had a letter telling me I have inherited a little property here outside Cannes!"

"Well I never! Are you sure someone is not playing a joke on you?"

"No. It is legitimate. Can I come over and show you?"

"Yes, of course."

It was a complete surprise and when Henry read it, he got out the map to see where about the property was located.

"It's just around this village somewhere."

In the letter there was the name of their Cannes representative, and he had the keys.

"Maybe the lawyers will take us."

Next morning, we were on their doorstep. They had the same letter from Australia and they had the leys! There was no one at the office to take us there, so I signed a few papers and we took the keys.

"We'll find it." Henry said as he had the maps with him. We started driving along the coast road going east, following the directions. Once outside Cannes, we found the area far less crowded than the expected crush.

After about twenty minutes, we notice the road that goes up into the mountains, which was marked on the map, and then found the fork in the road shortly afterwards. We then looked for signs because the houses were set back in the pine trees and it was difficult to see them. We drove into a small village and stopped the car to ask at the local bistro about the house, and yes, they knew where it was. Straight on to the left, where there is a large pine tree by the gate. We drove on and there it was. It was a beautiful location, surrounded by pine trees, and their scent drifted towards us. I had only one key plus the key for the padlock on the gate. We parked the car in the shade and walked to the gate. The padlock was rusty and I thought we would never get it open, however Henry had some oil in the back of his car and that did the trick.

There were signs of a lawn but overgrown, as were the shrubs on the path. There were cobwebs around the door. I suddenly wished that we had brought a handy man with us, to pry open doors and things. But there was no trouble getting the lock turned. There was a musty smell and we thought that the house couldn't have been occupied for years. The whole place was nearly derelict so we had difficulty walking through the place.

However when we opened the shutters in the living room, there was a breathtaking view of the sea below.

"Oh look Henry, look at the view. Come over here!" He came to the window.

We both looked down across the valley to the sea. It was sensational.

"How beautiful," I murmured. Fortunately I brought my camera so started taking photos of everything.

Walking through the house, I could see the possibilities, but it was all rather depressing with mold and rust everywhere. The bathroom would have to be redone as well as the kitchen, in fact, most of the house. It would take ages.

I walked out to the back of the house. There once was a garden and with a bit of work, I could plant some herbs over by the big gum tree. I could grow leeks, potatoes, lettuce and radishes and maybe some flowers. There was already a bay tree and a lemon tree. The ground looked good enough although everything was so overgrown, you could see that there was once a flower garden here. There were two rose bushes in the front and two at the back. .

We locked up and drove back down the hill, both silently thinking the same thoughts probably. A lot of work and a lot of money if I didn't want to sell it off immediately.

"I need a drink, can we stop somewhere." I asked. We stopped at the same bistro and sat outside. They were setting up the lunch tables, so we decided to have an early lunch and ask around about for any further details.

"The lunch is on me Henry. Today we are celebrating."

The woman proprietor seemed more knowledgeable than the man. Henry picked up their French easier than I did. It seems that my aunt used to come every year until about two years ago, then she had written to them, and asked them to try and rent the place out for her. I felt somehow pleased that I was talking to people who knew her and could tell us more about her.

They used to rent it out for her when she wasn't here.

There was a family who lived there last year so at least it had been occupied. But they moved on and in the winter nobody wanted the place. The electricity was turned off, and their letters to her, asking what she wanted to do, were never answered.

They spoke some English and so I could talk to them.

"I just heard that she died a few weeks ago."

"We thought that there must have been something wrong, we hadn't heard from her for so long. We are so sorry to hear that. We liked her very much. She loved it up here but she was always alone."

"Do you know if she had any friends around here?"

They didn't know unfortunately. Customers were sitting down at the tables, so they had to attend to them.

We had a delicious lunch of roast chicken and the trimmings washed down with a white local wine. I decided that it was going to be real risk if I renovated the place, if I would be able to sell it, after all it was well outside Cannes.

"Of course you will be able to sell it. You'll probably get a fortune for it."

"I will need a bank loan to do the renovations."

"Well with the price of property these days, you shouldn't have any problems"

"I wonder if a local bank will do it?"

"I'm sure one in Cannes will. You can try my bank. I know the Manager, and can vouch for you."

"First of all I'll have to find out how much it will cost"

The couple had said to call them Jean and Marie. So as we were leaving we asked them.

"Do you by any chance know of anyone who does renovations around here?"

I was lucky. Yes, there was a group just in the next town. they had their phone number and recommended them because they had renovated their kitchen last winter.

"Brilliant! Then could you recommend them?"

"Of course, they were very professional and fast and did exactly what we wanted."

They wanted to take us in to show us, so we went through the dining room to see the work. It looked good enough.

"They could come down and give you an estimate. Would you like me to phone them now?'

I looked at Henry. "Why not?" he shrugged.

It didn't take long. They were there. Madame spoke in rapid French, but I was able to understand her. They knew the house, and someone would meet us there in 45 minutes.

We went back to the patio and had another glass of cold white wine. It was a lovely day, not a cloud in the sky, a high wide sky. Somehow the skies in France seem higher, than in England. This was some kind of special day…a cottage, a village, in France. How often do these things happen? Not very often.

We were there when two men arrived in a truck. We shook hands all round, and I guess they thought that we were a couple and that Henry was my husband, because they addressed all their comments to him which was just as well as he could at least understand their local accents. I'm usually O.K. with Parisian French, but when there is an accent I am lost.

I kept adding comments as if I was the bossy wife. I'd like airconditioning, a dishwasher, washing machine and dryer. I thought that maybe only Americans would be able to afford the place after we had finished with it. I wanted to have it done properly.

They took measurements, they knocked on the walls, the floor, the pipes, the door frames and I wondered if they were going to send us a bill, after all it took nearly an hour. I wondered if I would be wise to get a second estimate from some other company, but they seemed to be honest enough. If the village people used them, they should be O.K.

They went back to the truck, and started writing out an estimate. I looked around the house again, and realized that the furniture was too mouldy to keep, that everything had to go. The Curtains, the carpet, the beds, and all the stuff in the drawers and closets. I presumed that the clothes that were left there were the last tenants possessions, and I wondered about the pictures on the wall. None of which were worth keeping. Total renovation was needed. The shutters would probably have to be replaced too because they were almost hanging off their hinges in some places.

The smell of the pine trees and the eucalyptus gum trees was absolutely divine. I loved it here but couldn't see living here alone. Henry had his own home, and besides we weren't in love even though we had become very fond of each other. I don't know how my aunt could have lived here on her own. I wondered what she did with her time, maybe the locals will know. Gardening maybe, which can take a lot of time and effort. If she didn't have a car and walked into the village for her provisions, then that would take most of the morning. The French like to shop every day. It even has a name your daily shopping. People ask you have you done your 'faire les courses'…that means your daily shopping. She may have spent the morning faisant les courses and then gardened in the afternoon and read at night. There was no television, but I noticed a battered old radio in the kitchen.

Finally they came back to us, and handed Henry their estimate. He read it without comment then handed it to me, They followed with an explanation that the new kitchen and bathroom had not included the new appliances. and that we would have to decide how much we wanted to spend on them. I was quite shocked at the price. It was high, well over twenty thousand pounds. With appliances and new furniture and new shutters we are looking at another ten thousand. But what was the alternative? I wanted to see it back in shape, and maybe by the time it was finished, I might have found a rich man who would live there with me.

Henry said he would phone his bank manager in the morning and we could go and see him for a loan.

That night in bed, I thought about my elderly aunt, who had been so generous. I really don't remember anything about her. I felt sad that we hadn't been in touch with her, and now she was dead. It is difficult to keep in touch, when everybody is living their own daily lives, to keep in touch with relatives overseas. How kind of her, she could have just left instructions to sell the place, but she didn't.

I felt I wanted to repay her somehow. But how? I wondered if she had had a favourite charity or her school perhaps? I wondered where she went to school. Isabelle. A pretty name. Never married. There had been five maiden school teachers in our family, who never married. It was probably something to do with the two world wars when so many of the young men had been killed in action and there were no eligible bachelors left. The carnage at Tripoli for example, hundreds of young men slaughtered and the battle of the Somme as well as the other horrific battles that people will never forget..at least not in our generation.

Next morning Henry and I went to see his bank manager. He was a close friend evidently, so it wasn't very difficult to arrange a loan, with Henry as the guarantor. I opened a bank account there because I knew I would need funds from home to help buy every thing else. It was rather nice to think I had a French bank account, as if I was now a resident. I also has some final papers to sign with regard to the house which needed a banker's signature to send back to the lawyers.

The men started work on the house the following week. I went up to take photographs inside and outside, before they started. I hoped that the 'before' photos and hopefully show what the 'after' photos would cost. Fortunately the roof and wiring didn't need to be fixed, it was really just the interiors. The floor surfaces needed to be replaced and some of the walls. Plastering was something that I had never tried. It was rather exciting to think that they could make this place livable. I wandered around looking at the overgrown garden, trying to distinguish if any of the plants were reviveable. There were two rose bushes by the gate, so I could prune those and maybe they would survive. Otherwise it looked like it would have to be all replanted. I could use lots of pots, geraniums always look good. The place would look great after it had been painted.

I asked Henry where he had bought his furniture and household things, and he took me to a shop just outside Cannes, rather like a Monoprix and everything was there.

Sofas, beds, carpets, sheets and towels, it would be easy enough to buy it all there when the house was finished. I began to feel that it would be such a joy to fix it up and play house that I might want to keep it for myself. The taxes I found out later were astronomical for such a tiny property, but this is the Alps Maritimes so what can you expect. I started to make a list of everything that needed to be bought, down to a bathroom mat and shower curtain to match. Being only one bedroom, it was an easy decision as to furniture. There would be a bed sofa for the living room, just in case there was need of a second bed.

I asked the men to extend the tiny patio at the back, and make it quite large, so I could put a table and chairs out there, and make it outdoor dining room under the gum trees. In this part of the world, you need to be able to eat outdoors. It occurred to me that Isabelle must have wanted this too, but maybe she just came here in the winter. Yes, it is summer in Australia, very hot, when it is winter here, so that's is probably when she came over..during the long summer school holidays. January and February.

I was determined to continue with the writing and even though every morning I wanted to jump out of bed, and drive up to the house, I contained myself and wrote for two hours after my walk along the beach..

Then after a quick lunch, usually soup and a sandwich I would call Henry to see what he was doing, ask him if he wanted to drive up to the house with me, or not and depending on his answer, I would either go alone or with him. He didn't want to go every day, and I could understand that. Sometimes if it was raining I didn't go either. But

I wanted to watch what the workmen were doing and suggest things as they went along. I usually stopped by the village and often did my grocery shopping up there to save time.

It was approaching mid-summer, so the days were getting hot by noon. I knew that it would be hotter up there, so I went to the beach for a swim if it was too hot to drive.

I worked in the garden when it was cooler, and as long as I didn't get in their way, the workmen watched me as they walked between the truck and the house carrying in the supplies. The undergrowth of bushes and hedges really needed cutting back, and I borrowed some tools from them. A saw was needed to get rid of the toughest parts. It was hard work and I scratched my hands badly one day when I was determined to get rid of some prickly stuff. I went down to the village and bought some gloves that I should have had at the beginning. There were no signs of any flowers, so I bought some pots and geraniums but it was rather useless to place them in front of the house until it had been painted. I wanted it cream with a white trim, white shutters against cream and white geraniums would look good I thought.

There was a lovely magnolia tree at the side of the house, just outside the bedroom window, so the perfume would no doubt be smelt inside on summer nights. Magnolias always seem to smell stronger at night. There was a lemon tree, but a very old one, and a crab apple…not much good for anything really. The lawn would have to be replanted, but maybe I would have it cemented over so I could use more chairs out there and have a barbecue perhaps. Less maintenance than a lawn A lawn mower was nowhere to be seen.

Each day driving back into Cannes I tried to imagine if I could live up there, on my own, and be happy. It was not something I had expected to happen. I usually have a plan, or plans, each year of what and where I will be. This was so different.

Henry and I went down to the old town for dinner that night, and I started to talk about it.

"I wonder if I could really live up there?"

'Well you could call it fate, I suppose. How often does someone inherit a cottage in the south of France.?"

"Do you believe that?"

"Believe what?"

"That it is fate?"

"I don't know. It does seem a kind of a sign. Maybe it is time to give up one life and start another."

"Like what?"

"Like living down here. Writing, learning French."

"I know French"

"Not really. You watch the BBC news not the French news"

" Yes. But that's not enough to keep the mind alive."

"You have to adapt. If you live in your little house, you can entertain, meet new friends, there are Brits all over the place down here, back in the woods if you like, because that's where they like to be. I happen to like being down here near the beach and the action."

They go to the supermarket and the wine shop and congregate together at the local bistro reacting a former existence, then speak with nostalgia and authority of the Riviera.

"I don't think I could find enough to do."

"You keep writing, that's what you do"

"I think I better find a back-up, just in case."

"It is really up to you."

"Mind you, the peace and tranquillity is wonderful. It reminded me of when our parents took us camping and there was such a great silence after the sun had gone down. The birds were quiet, only the occasional owl, the tent was a wonderful place to lie in the dark and breathe the soft air of summer. It actually reminded me of being very young again, somehow the quietness was reminding me of my youth. London was so noisy now, I had started noticing it months ago, the buses and the trucks screeching at you going by.

It was a lovely sunset again tonight, I felt as if I wanted to invite all my friends down here, but I knew from past experience that not all of them liked it here, and if they couldn't speak the language they disliked it even more.

Henry was trying to cope every day, without his wife. I could tell that she had been the one who kept him busy with activities and running errands each day so now he was really lost so I tried to help him as much as I could.

"Why don't we drive to Nice today, and go to that English bookshop. It reminds me a little of Hatchards because they have all the latest books, and it is impossible to leave without buying one. I don't read about all the new books, but when you go there, you discover them and it is like Christmas time."

'That's a good idea. We could have lunch at La Gougaline" His demeanor changed immediately.

He deliberately mispronounced the name of one of our favorite places, a restaurant just this side of Nice, which was right on the beach. We usually went there at night, because it was lovely to see the sunset and the reflections on the water, the rose coloured hue of the sand. It was not a place that tourists knew about and usually residents kept it to themselves. During dinner, the waiters sing operatic arias, as they served you dinner. The mood was festive, cheerful and everybody seemed to enjoy the whole experience..

"We haven't been there for ages. I love that place." We both like places which are near or on the water.But now I was busy up in the bush every day.

Unfortunately when we got there, the place was closed for renovations, so we went into Nice. The bookshop was open and sure enough there were many new books, fresh new biographies we hadn't heard of which we snapped up. We could give them to our local library when we had read them. Our library would get them eventually but not for another six months or so. It was our main source of reading and we were very protective of it. I suggested to Henry that he work there as a volunteer so he was still thinking about that.

Each day I drove up to the little cottage. Anyone who has ever hired contractors to do renovations knows what kinds of problems arise. I wasn't going to be spared. They were efficient enough, but made mistakes , expensive mistakes, until I wondered if it was the language barrier which was the problem. They made the counters in the kitchen to go on the opposite side from where they were now. Why? They said because of the plumbing, and the pipes but surely if the old ones were in place, but they decided if that's where I wanted them, that would be O.K. but it would cost more. And so it went on.

Driving back we were terrified when a car in front of us just veered off the road, and went crashing through a fence. It stopped just before it hit a building and there was a cliff just beyond it. We pulled over in the car, and got out. A man opened the door, the driver and waved to us. We stopped by the fence and shouted.

"Are you all right?"

He accepted a ride into the next village after inspecting the damage. He turned out to be British, and was trying to find a British couple who had bought a place further on. He called them on his cell and told them the news. I was surprised to see him looking hard at me as I turned around from the front seat,

"Didn't you used to be Nicole Bennett?"

"Oh hell.. Not only did he recognize me, but he immediately classified me as ancient.

"Used to be?" I smiled. I thought of Dirk Bogarde who wrote that he used to get that all the time from taxi drivers in London.

"Sorry. I meant aren't you Nicole Bennett" He laughed. I didn't find it very amusing. But then it was my choice to retire from the business. I had steeled myself from these kind of remarks because in the beginning they came from all over. It hurt at first, like the pulling off a band aid from your skin, or large bandage but soon swiftly disappears.

We approached the next village and he insisted on buying us a drink at the pretty little cafe under the trees. It was Henry who accepted.

"Yes, thank you." He nodded to me as if he wanted to. I would have declined because I knew he'd want to question me further.

"What's your name?" asked Henry

"Tony. Tony Harwood." And yours? I know Nicole's"

"Henry Morehead."

"You both have been incredibly helpful. I owed you a drink and besides I'll have to wait here for my friends.

As the waiter put our drinks down on the table, I managed to have a good look at him, as he reached into his wallet to pay. He was very handsome actually, slim, well over six feet, around 160 lbs I would have thought, with bushy brown hair and a rather good skin. Tanned and with brown eyes. His clothes were rather worn, but then he was on holiday I expect. A leather jacket that had seen better days, and a yellow button down shirt. His hands were long and tanned. I felt a little twinge of desire. Oh dear. I bet he is in the business I thought. It had been a long time since I had felt anything like I was feeling now.

"Well here's to my new found friends" he lifted his glass and smiled at both of us.

"Cheers" we answered. Oh dear, why does that always sound so British, we are in France after all.

If I had said "A votre sante." he may have thought I was putting on airs. So why not? We should at least try to familiarize ourselves with the local customs. I think this village must be used to the British. A little like Chianti-shire in Italy.

"What happened back there?" asked Henry.

"Well I suppose I was going too fast and I leant over to try to read the directions on the map and ran off the road. I know if you take your eyes off the road for a second it can happen, but I thought the road was straight enough to do it."

"We thought that you must have had a flat tire, or something."

"Well I hope someone can fix the bloody thing"

It was a rental car, and he had already phoned the rental car company to advise them where the car was, and that they should bring him another one to the address where he could be staying. I don't want to wait here all day until they show up, he explained.

There was a definite frisson between us and I hoped that Henry hadn't noticed. Not that he would've minded but it seemed rather inappropriate.

"I was sorry to hear about your loss." Tony said.

"Thank you. It was a terrible shock at the time, but as they say, time is supposed to heal everything." I was polite but screaming inside at the cliché. No!time does not heal everything. Why am I still dreaming about that bastard Michael? I can't control my dreams, so why doesn't good old time do something about it. Time has nothing to do with it. Crazy idiot me.

"Can I be so bold as to ask if you are going back to show business?" he smiled a really lovely smile.

Oh God, look at him, I thought. Another heart breaker, and another headache. Why am I such a dummy. A beautiful smile, for a handsome man, why can't I learn?

"No. I gave it up years ago."

"Oh come off it, it wasn't so long ago. I loved you in that last movie you did."

"I have retired. I hate those early morning calls, I always loathed them. It is extremely tiring and after a while if you don't need the lolley, why bother?"

"But you are so talented."

Henry was listening to us and looked rather bewildered as I hadn't really talked to him at all about my career. He will want to see my movies I know and then it will be all questions. I had been very careful not to talk about Michael, only Nigel so he was again rather surprised when Tony said

"And that fabulous writer you lived with, Michael…what's his name. He was so brilliant and clever. I met him here at the Cannes Festival once. He had a film here."

"Yes, I know. That's when I met him too." I looked at him closely. My heart started pounding, this was getting too close for comfort. He must have been in Cannes the same time I was here. He probably was at the same party that Michael gave, and where I first fell in love with him. Just hearing someone say his name made me tremble. Well he didn't remember his last name, thank goodness and I wasn't about to tell him. Wait for it, he is going to tell you exactly that. Oh dear, do I need this?.

"Were you by any chance at that fabulous party he gave after the showing? He had everybody there. He was such a popular fellow. You must have been there."

"How long has it been since you've seen him? That party must have been ten years ago. I know he had a surprise wedding which nobody knew about. You went off with someone else I seem to remember. I guess you heard that they had a child?"

A knife went through me. Bang. I froze with the pain. Shocked, I hope it didn't show in my face. I'm an actress aren't I? Well, now is the time, if anytime was apt, play your part, Nicole, act and speak as normal.

"No I hadn't heard." I managed to get out. 'We really didn't keep in touch"

Christ what agony. A child? A boy or a girl. My question was answered.

"A boy I think. He said he wanted more. But I haven't heard."

"Neither have I" Quicky I picked up my purse and said

"Sorry I must spend a penny." And walked swiftly inside to the loo.

Under my breath in my head, the old hymn started."Oh God, our help in ages past, our hopes for years to come. He shelters us from stormy blasts..." something like that anyway. I shut the door to the loo. I had to get away from the table I couldn't sit there any longer. I looked in the mirror and let the news sink in. So they had a child. Bully for them. I hope it was ugly, that it screamed through the night, kept them awake for hours, I hope it was a wretched baby who was miserable and fretful. Now, I knew it, the old nonsense, a huge empty feeling in the pit of my stomach. Oh dear. He would never consider having a child when we were together. We were too busy, we were too young, I don't think we even discussed it although we must have sometime. I don't remember. How could he? How could he? The whole bloody stuff started all over again.

However I couldn't stay for ever in the loo.

I heard a car pull up and voices so I guess it was his friends. I should go out again. We would have no more exchanges about Michael.

He was introducing Henry to two friends, Dianne and David. He turned to me, and then turned back to them and said..

"And this is Nicole..Nicole Bennett. Remember she was in that marvelous film and won the Oscar. She was living with that wonderful writer... the one who was an Earl or Baron or something

"Hi there" They didn't react thank God.

We shared a drink together and they told us about their decision to leave England and come and buy a house here five years ago. They were very happy and had no regrets. They were very polite but I could see that they were trying to figure out Henry and I and our relationship. At least we knew that they were a couple.

Finally they finished their drinks and they strolled over to their car.

We exchanged phone numbers and I said we must keep in touch.

Driving back to Cannes I asked Henry what he had thought of them. "Well there are hundreds of Brits down here now, I think because the climate is so much better than England and the pleasures of living so much easier, I can understand it."

"But the Brits don't like the French, that's well known. I wonder how they manage with their attitude."

"I suppose it is like the Americans. The French don't like them either."

"I am constantly amazed because they seem so prejudiced. Maybe because they know that without the Yanks, we all would be speaking German."

"You know they don't want to recognize that. They have deliberately forgotten on purpose. One of my friends married a Frenchman and they live in Paris. They have a 14 year old who goes to school there. One day he showed his mother his history book, and she was surprised to see that the Free French liberated Paris, there was not a word about Eisenhower or the US troops. She, being an American, was appalled."

"I think sooner or later we will have to set them right."

"I only resent the French when they pretend that they can't understand when I try to talk to them. They really do, you know."

The evening was turning into a pale pearl pink across the sky, like the inside of an oyster shell.

" Oh! How beautiful. I adore this place."

"Nicole, who is Michael? When Tony mentioned his name to you, I noticed your reaction. Your face was as white as a sheet."

"Oh just a man I used to know, that's all"

"You are being a little unfair Nicole. There is a lot you haven't told me about your life, and then some stranger mentions someone, who must have been tremendously important in your life, and whom I know nothing about."

He was hurt. As if I had deliberately kept something from him, which of course, I had.

"Well actually Henry, it is still so painful to talk about it. I came here hoping to forget that part of my life, and talking about it makes it harder."

"Well it makes me feel a bit of a fool, when these people seem to know more about your career and your private life than I do."

"No. don't feel that way. I am trying to forget my past life. You are part of my new life, it is that simple. I just want to forget the painful times, that's all."

"Well at least you could tell me who this Michael is or was. Is that too much?"

So I told him. I tried to be very matter of fact, as if it really didn't matter anymore.

"I first met Michael in Cannes, he was producing a movie and I went to the opening reception. We moved in together when we went back to London. He wrote a film script and managed to get me the lead part. Don't ask, but it happened. Unfortunately the film had to be shot in Los Angeles, so I went there and stayed for six months. Michael was tied up in London and could only get over every six weeks or so. He said we would be married when the film was finished. I missed him terribly, as I was deeply in love with him. Well when the film finished, and I came back he had changed. I didn't know what it was, but he was different. What it was, I found out later, was another woman in his life. Things became complicated because I had been nominated for an Oscar, and they wanted me to go back to California for the Awards night. I said I would, only because Michael said he would come with me.

Henry had slowed down and was driving quite slowly, as he listened to me. I thought that perhaps he had heard enough. We were both watching the road, as we talked. So there was no eye contact at all.

"Go on," he said. "What happened?" His voice was not hostile as it had been a few moments earlier.

"Well after all the planning, Michael didn't show up. He phoned and left a message that his flight had been delayed. I went to the Awards with my agent, instead."

Henry turned off the side road, to get onto the highway so I waited until he had made the turn.

"How much more do you want?" I asked him.

"You must have been very upset."

That was the understatement of the year. Not only did he not show up, I was devastated to hear what had happened.

"Well?"

"My close friend had gone around to our apartment to check and she found a note from him, saying he had left, and he was getting married the next day. He would explain when I got back."

"What a bastard." Henry said, and I was surprised at his concern.

"Yes, well there you have it. He had disappeared when I got home. He never did explain. His clothes were gone from the flat, and he left no forwarding address."

We drove on for a few minutes in silence. I really didn't want to go on with re-telling the story, but may as well finish the whole saga.

He blamed it all on our separation. If I hadn't gone to L.A. etc. He had asked me not to go, but I really wanted the part, and I trusted him because we loved each other

"I think we need a drink after all this. I'll try and get parking by the Carlton."

So there we were back on the terrace, sitting facing the sea.

After our drinks came he sat in silence for awhile then said,

"What did you do?"

"It was humiliating. I started searching for him. He wasn't in London so I went to Capri, because he told me he had a small house there. But he wasn't there. It took me weeks to actually calm down. My friends helped. I worked a lot on some TV shows, so I had to stop searching for him."

Love is so painful when it is tied up with sexual passion. I swore I would never become so vulnerable again. He kept saying that he loved me, that he wanted to marry me, and I believed him!

"Why shouldn't you?"

Because he was a pathological liar. It took ages to get over him. When I was in Capri I met a friend of his who helped me try and find him. Michael wasn't on the island, so I waited a week or two. Peter was very helpful.

"Peter? I haven't heard about him, have I?"

"No."

"So what happened to him?"

"A long story..he came back to London after a few weeks, and we saw a lot of each other then. I didn't want to go into that relationship. Too soon to talk about it really I just said we had to wait.

"And?".

"He was killed in a car crash. It was about a year after we met."

Another silence.

We sat there, looking at the view that we both had become so attached to, it was a place that was so peaceful at times, you couldn't imagine the madness of when the Film Festival was on.

"Getting back to Michael…did you ever see him again?"

"Yes, after Peter died. One day he rang me, and we met, but it was obviously a duty call."

Suddenly a cold breeze blew over the terrace.

"Oh, that's chilly. I didn't bring a jacket." We quickly finished our drinks and left.

That night I dreamt of Michael. Those days had come back. Hell. I thought they had gone. How can I get him out of my dreams I wondered. How do people do that? I wish I knew. It occurred to me that some men like Michael know how to please and entertain a woman… they may not love them, but they make a woman happy. Both in bed and out of it. Whereas someone like Henry, if he said he loved you, he really meant it. That is always a compliment, which women fall for. Some men can really love, but some of them don't know how to please a women. Maybe a little like Henry. He is really a dull man, with hardly any sense of humor or fun, and I am sure his wife found him so, but she put up with it, because he loved and respected her.

Chapter Nine

We didn't mention Michael or Peter again after that. He knew I didn't want to relive all that again and I was busy trying to get my life in order and the house in order. Henry began to take interest in my project... It was a shame really that we had no physical chemistry because he was such a good companion.

"Do you want to go and see where Edith Wharton's house is? She lived there for years and so many illustrious people visited her there."

"Where is it?" I asked. It was curious because I always thought that she had lived in Paris.

"Down towards Hyeres."

"Well that's not far. West of here, I remember I went through it on the train.

"It was also where Queen Victoria stayed too…she loved the place, it seems."

It was great to have Henry help me. It added something to the occasion; a drink or a meal knowing that you might be sitting in the same wicker chair that one of these people had sat in. Dirk Bogarde must have been slightly nostalgic too, because he wrote in one of his letters, after the death of Natalie Wood that he missed seeing her sitting on her regular bar stool at the bar at the Colombe d'Or. She used to come every year and there is a photo of her sitting on Dirk's terrace with him. He entertained many women including Glenda Jackson, Jane Birkin and her daughter Charlotte Gainsborough. Kathleen Tynan, Penelope Mortimore, all photographed on his terrace. He writes that the house was entirely booked with houseguests during the summer months.

Oh time, what a time, when all is gone, just like the time I was at Blue Harbour, Noel Coward's house in Jamaica. It was so moving to be there, even if it was only to imagine Coward being there.

Dirk's letters are very entertaining. He writes one day, that his novel was not going well, that he had all his characters up in a plane, but inspiration had left him. The solution? "I feel like crashing the plane and there will be no survivors..not one."

The ordeal of creating each day made me realize just how difficult writing is. At one time his companion, Tony started a book and Dirk was amused to see how difficult Tony found starting it.

We went back to talking about visiting these places.

"So I am too sentimental, too nostalgic I suppose. But why then, do people visit other sites, if not literary, such as where Picasso worked and Chagall.?"

"I didn't say a word." smiled Henry.

We were sitting in a café in the centre of a village where Coco Chanel used to shop.

"How about cemeteries…they are even worse. I would like to go to the cemetery in Menton where Aubrey Beardsley is buried. Imagine he died when he was 25." I had looked him up before I left London. What a genius. His life was so short but he left us all those fantastic drawings."

'We'll go one day and see if we can find it. I hear it is a rather large place."

It was. The day we went there it took as over an hour to find his grave. The view from the cemetery was worth the climb, overlooking the coast and the glittering blue sea beyond. He deserved such a picturesque resting-place.

The work on the little cottage was slow. In the meantime I kept shopping for all the things it would need. Pots and pans, china, glassware, cutlery and everything for the kitchen which was sometimes fun but always stressful dealing with the shopkeepers in frog. Henry was happy enough to store all the stuff at his place, as he had a storage place in his basement. When it was finished I would either rent it out, or sell it. I knew I would be much too lonely to live in it by myself. When I think about all the times I felt lonely when I was on location, it was inevitable that I didn't want more of the same thing. Of course, there were lots of British living around the place, only several miles way, but would I be able to work there, day after day, alone? I liked cooking but it is really no fun to cook for one.

One day Henry asked me if I would like to have dinner with some old friends of his who had an apartment in the old part of Cannes.

"They are French, and don't speak much English. There is a rather glamorous mother, and her adult son, who lives with her. He likes to restore antique furniture and I think makes quite a good living at it. Just for a change, I thought it might be pleasant."

Well it was one of the most boring evenings I have spent. Poor old Henry, I think he was a bit keen on the woman. She was a certain age, around 60 I would think. Very French, very cultivated, very sophisticated and obviously with a great interest in clothes. She looked me up and down when we were greeted at the door. I realized that she is the kind of woman who judges you by your clothes. If you were wearing designer clothes, she would know which designer I thought. However she seemed to approve of me, I must admit I had worn one of my best outfits. But the evening went nowhere. I couldn't image their lives. She was so typical French, very disciplined and soignée as only the French woman can be, I guessed she spent a lot of time with her dressmaker and tailor for the son. He was watching Henry like a hawk as I think he felt threatened. Another man in his home possibly? We went to a local restaurant, again very French, only the locals would be able to find it I thought. Not a tourist in sight. I found it a strain to keep conversing in French when I found little to talk to these people about. When I told them I was an actress they looked as if I was from out of space. Perhaps they had never met one. I felt sorry for Henry if these were the kind of friends he had. I think that they were friends of his late wife, because there was no connection at all.

We drove back in silence. I said the usual stuff. Interesting people and thank you for inviting me, the food was great. He dropped me at my door, and we said goodnight.

Later lying in bed, I groaned with the thought of the evening. How many hundreds of women in the world like her? Not just in France, but everywhere. They seem to be content. Maybe they are, but I couldn't believe it. What's wrong with me? Why can't I be like her, a normal woman. Taking care of her adult son, who didn't seem to be that bright, but of course knows which side his bread is buttered on, and will probably never leave her. They live quiet, simple lives, the daily life rather better than their English counterparts, as at least the weather is better, but they don't feel restless, or uninspired, or frustrated. I wished it were so simple. Year after year, they celebrate the family's Fête days, or the French Fête days, in the fact that they have so many rituals, more so if you have a large family. I felt depressed at the thought. No wonder Gauguin left for Tahiti and paint, leaving France forever. Or like some French student I once met in Paris, who became obsessed with studying the lives of the red Indians, the poux rouges.. He left his wife and two children to take a course, at a mid western US university for two years. It was soon after my arrival in France and at a cocktail party he kept talking about 'the peaux rouges' until it finally dawned on me that he was speaking about red Indians.

I kept thinking of that idea until I fell asleep. Henry didn't ask me to meet anymore of his friends after that.

Chapter Ten

Again, Bogarde's letters were my daily reading during this time. Witty, interesting, clever and very funny, they eased the pain of trying to write. His books and letters seem effortless, so it is kind of therapeutic to read when you are trying to write yourself.

Most how-to books about writing say that you should never write about how you are feeling. I find that odd. I liked to read about how people are feeling. Maybe it is boring to most people but when writers write that nothing is coming on the page, then you don't feel quite so lost anymore. He did it all the time. Staring at a blank piece of paper.

I wonder if you don't ever move from your own hometown whether you are happier throughout your life. It is a thought, because then you don't know anything better. You have family, friends, rituals, comforts, and lots of people who know you, whether they love you or not is another matter. It is the age-old question. I certainly couldn't have stayed in my hometown. It was a throw back from some distant relative or gene… travelust or ambition, whatever. You either have it in your bones or you don't.

Now I was here, I realized that sometime one has to settle down, but I didn't know where to go. Dirk found his spiritual home here, just a few miles away, and he adored being there. I knew that from his letters. Paris has the same effect on me, but this place is almost as wonderful. The only thing is that if your muse is not happening, then you are not in the right place.

Villefranche is along the coast road but there is a rather sharp turn to get to the harbor, and many people miss it. It took me several attempts to find my way down the steep road that leads to the picturesque harbor and the famous old Welcome Hotel that is right in the forefront of the village. It really should be called the Writer's Hotel, because so many famous writers have stayed there and worked there. Many people know about Cocteau living there, and painting the famous chapel in the village, but others don't know that the hotel was their meeting place for generations.

Cocteau lived on the second floor of the hotel for over ten years and he welcomed many contemporaries who came to stay. Writers, artists, musicians, their presence making the village almost an artist's retreat, they all met at the nearby cafes and bistros each evening. Diaghilev, Nijinski, Colette, Bakst all stayed here.

We sat in the small town square where there were many little restaurants to choose from, for lunch. The past seemed very present. I remember reading a novel, which took place at the Welcome Hotel about a couple who decided to have a second honeymoon at the hotel. At the last minute, the husband was delayed by work and she went alone. She met a wonderful Frenchman, had a passionate affair, and when the husband arrived he caught them in the room, and stormed out. The novel ended with the fact that the husband wouldn't allow her to return home with him, not that she wanted to, he divorced her, and she ended up becoming a penniless laundress back in London, after the affair died out. What a warning I thought. It sounded too close to reality.

Evelyn Waugh, the British author who wrote many well known novels, including the famous 'Brideshead Revisited" stayed at the hotel numerous times. He first came with his brother, Alec Waugh, who at the time was more celebrated than Evelyn but they soon parted company. In 1931 he wrote from there that "the district is full of chums, Cyril Connolly, Aldous Huxley, Eddie Sackville West, too literary by half."

"I'm too old for self discovery," I laughed. "Or rather I discovered myself, and got fed up with what I saw years ago!" I decided that helping other people is the best thing I can be doing at anytime. I think I am helping Henry recover from one of the most traumatic events in his life, and of course he is helping me. Every so often you have to get away to recharge your batteries so you can go on helping people. It is this darned 'creative impulse' wanting to create, to paint, to act, to write, it is something you cannot shake. Reading about all the great painters who came down here and struggled for years makes you wonder though. Most of them, except of course for Picasso, did not become famous until after their deaths. They could have been miserable anywhere, so why not in one if the beautiful places on earth. The other artists who stayed in Paris or other parts of Europe, suffered too. Painters particularly seemed to be the most poverty strickened. Perhaps because they had to buy paints, canvases ad brushes all the time, whereas writers only needed paper in those days.

The sun was slowly going down and the sky was high. The colors of the sunset would appear soon, blazing red with rays of yellow, pink, gold across the sky. Wouldn't it be wonderful if we could see this all year round, some place else, like dreary old Manchester or in the depths of some awful place.

"Well I'm sure they have great sunsets in Manchester" he laughed.

"Once in a blue moon. I was brought up there, so I happen to know."

Chapter Eleven

Tony decided to try and see Nicole again because he knew her work, and he realized that she was probably lonely if she was alone down here. Henry had filled him in outside while Nicole was in the bathroom at the roadside restaurant and he thought that he maybe able to help. He had been through the loss of a job, a wife and child, so he was very much on his own. His thoughts were racing ahead.....I am going to see her again, no matter what, he said to himself. Why not? If I play my cards right, she might decide to let me stay in her new little cottage, he thought. I maybe a bit of an adventurer, but I know what I want. Even if she didn't take to him right away he could be very charming and persuasive, he thought.

"Your God's gift to women" laughed his mother years ago, when he told her that he could interest most girls who weren't so attractive to him.

June thought so too. But wasn't going to let on. He was far too spoilt already.

That evening he phoned me, I wasn't in but he left a message and asked me to call. I guess he thought that I would if I wanted to see him again, and if not that was it. Well after a few more messages I guess he gave up. So I had won my battle.

Now I've got Henry and John for company, I don't need another guy hanging around. Especially as he is a temptation, and one I don't need to get involved with, that's for sure. I told Pauline after tennis that day.

I remembered that book called All Passion Spent. well that's exactly how I felt. I will read and will eat and I want no more feelings of lust, or temptations, of fighting. Just peace, it is sexual passion that is so exhausting, and so wasted.

"I don't want to get involved with someone like him. It was too dangerous. It means that I could easily fall in love again, and then it would be too late. The easiest thing is not to see him again." I explained to her.

So it was easy not to return his calls. I thought that in two weeks he would be gone and I waited patiently for those two weeks to be over. No more temptation.

"Have I grown so old that I don't care anymore?" I asked Pauline as if she would know. "No, you've just grown up."

When Henry and I went out for a picnic the next week to a spot near Antibes, I discussed Tony with him and he agreed that he was not the person I should be involved with. I loved him for that, and thought that close friendship, without sex, is probably a much better relationship for me, or for any one for that matter, who gets too emotionally and physically upset when things go wrong. Nobody likes rejection and I'd certainly have had my share of it.

That night I couldn't sleep. I lay in the dark, going over all that had lead up to this flight to France. I had told Henry that evening most of the rest of the story, and I thought back to exactly what I had told him.

"I know you are curious about why I split up with my husband and I should tell you because you have been so understanding and supportive. You maybe able to help."

"If you think so."

"Well I first met him when a group of us were staying on holiday in Jamaica, at Noel Coward's old house, Blue Harbor. He was a next door neighbor and came over for drinks one night."

"That sounds most romantic."

"It was. He had lost his wife, a year or two earlier, and used to help the owner of Blue Harbor if there were any difficulties. Without going into too many details, he was there when we needed him. I saw a great deal of him, and we used to go swimming together. Well we both fell in love. It sounds corny doesn't it?"

"No, quite natural I suppose."

"I mean really in love."

Henry waved the waitress over to order another brandy.

He seemed interested so I continued, watching for signs of boredom.

"I was recovering from losing Michael and he was recovering from his wife's death. We knew that we had both fallen in love and it was only a matter of time before we would be together, either in Jamaica or London."

"Anyway it turned out that he has a 20 year old son, Charles, in London who hadn't been in touch for quite awhile. He was worried, especially as the son hadn't come out when his mother was so ill, and made some excuse not to go there for her funeral either."

"Rather rotten of the son, I'd say."

"So I offered to help when we returned to London. Help find him and perhaps meet him. Then the day he took us all to the airport, he gave me the son's e mail and asked me to see him."

"He is about to go to Germany with a Rock Group instead of going on to University. I am coming over to London in two weeks to see what I can do." Evidently Nigel had told Charles about me, and surprisingly he said he'd love to meet me, as he had seen most of my movies. So it was all settled.

"I will be in London in two weeks Nicole." He whispered as he said goodbye to all of us at the airport.

I had an idea. "In the meantime would you like me to see him? I'd like to meet him very much."

"Yes, that would be great. He knows who you are as I told him all about you. In fact, he was going to suggest it but I didn't know what you would think about it."

"I'd love to meet him."

Chapter Twelve

Back in London I phoned him a few days later, and invited him for lunch at Kettners in Soho. I got there early, to get a good table at the back. I knew him right away. He had the same dark hair as Nigel, the blue eyes, tall and lanky.

I waved to him, from my table. He came over and smiled, as he had no trouble recognizing me. He sat down and kept smiling. He seemed like a charming person and it was amazing to think of all the dreadful hurtful things he had done to both his parents. I knew it was better to meet him this way.

"The lunch is on me,' I said, "So don't hold back. The menu here seems very good. I am always on a diet, but I'm sure you don't need to worry about calories. So please good ahead with anything you'd like." I was ordering a salad but I knew he might want more than that.

The lunch lasted two hours. I tried to stay off the subject of his parents, of Jamaica, and everything else that might annoy him. We talked mostly about music and music groups, who he had worked with, who he wanted to work with, who he admired most and lots of artists we had a mutual love for. I wanted him to like me, as I felt he might feel I was

Interfering in not only his life but his father's life, not that he cared much about that.

I invited him to a concert the following day, and we met for a drink beforehand. Again, he was very pleasant and I was beginning to think that he just maybe very lonely. He didn't seem to have a girfriend although just because he had mentioned anyone didn't mean that he didn't. We made arrangements to go to Ronnie Scott's that Saturday, as there were some musicians he knew.

Afterwards when we were walking back towards the Underground, he finally started to open up to me. I held my breath and was careful not to interrupt him. We stood by the tube entrance and he started to tell me about his early life. I said, "Look there's a wine bar over there, let's have a nightcap shall we?"

Thank goodness, the place was not crowded. We bought some crisps and peanuts to have with our drinks.

I suppose it is a well known fact that members of a family can talk to an outsider far more easily than within the family especially about their family problems. I found Charles a very well mannered boy or rather man, but Nigel had told me how abusive and rude he had been to him and his late wife, and as yet I hadn't seen a trace of it. It was as if he was another person. So far, he liked me and thought I was intelligent after solving all those mysteries on TV no doubt, but he genuinely seemed to like me. I couldn't hold out much longer about asking him about his mother. We had another couple of drinks, and then I said.

"Where do you think you got this talent and interest in music from? Is your Dad musical?"

"No not really. I guess it was from my mother. She insisted on music lessons for me."

"Tell me about your Mum?' Do you miss her? He suddenly became rigid and stared at me angrily. Wow, did I say the wrong thing.

His whole body language changed, he became a stranger. He shut down completely.

"Oops, sorry" I said. Trying to backtrack to our former jovial mood. I didn't mean to pry. I just thought that you might be able to tell me about your first love of music. I was shocked at his change of mood. It was if I had suddenly switched to talking about a murder, or as if I had stabbed him accidentally.

He looked angry still.

"Never mind, don't mind me, I just thought that as we were talking about music you might describe how you got started."

He wanted to talk I could see that. but he was so caught up with emotion coupled with rage, I didn't know what to say next. I have always prided myself on being able to smooth over awkward situations, and try to get back some of the friendliness of people, but this was something else. How could I get him to talk about it? Nigel had said that he had tried to get therapists to talk to him but it was all still bottled up inside. Rage, it was sheer rage against his mother. I was appalled at the strength of it. Oh dear what to be done but just go ahead with it. Go with the flow.

"I would really like to know why you feel so hostile towards your mother, after all you said she did instill the love of music in you."

Then it all came out. He started quite calmly. As if he had already rehearsed what he would say. Maybe he knew that Nigel had told me about their disapproval of each other so he was going to tell me why. It went back as early as when he was seven, just as Nigel had guessed. He never forgot the trauma of being left at Prep school by his mother. He loved her so, you could say, adored her and was so happy to be at home, with their animals, Fletcher their dog, Ebony, their cat and he loved their home and garden. Suddenly he was left into a kind of cruel place. Nobody loved him nobody cared, they just shouted orders, and told him to get on with it. He was cold, and nearly always hungry, uncomfortable and lonely. There were bullies, who mocked him, for being a sissy, and he begged his mother to take him back home.

I watched him as he spoke and he was choked up with emotion. After all these years! I was astonished as his pain, his vivid description and I think he was absolutely in earnest

He told me that he was abused sexually and that made me feel angry too.

"Why didn't you say something?" I said

"Who too? The masters would have laughed at me…as they were sleeping around I know with the head prefect or some other boy and I had no one to talk to. I was embarrassed. I couldn't possibly tell my parents, it was too much of a risk as they may not have believed it, and I would have been too humiliated to tell them."

I thought only a child would reason like that. Nevertheless it had happened, and for all I know might still be happening. The whole system seems so medieval and cruel. It obviously affects these boys for the rest of their lives. Nigel was right in saying that the book about the training of some regiments of the Guards is cruel and barbaric probably built on the treatment they got when in these Prep schools.

So now I had found out why he was so hostile. Was it too late to convince him that his parents were not to blame? That his mother, who obviously deeply loved him had no idea that this trauma would affect their relationship for the rest of their lives? Why, in this day and age, does this habit still exist I wonder? I don't know, all I know is that I have to convince this young man that his mother was unaware of the hurt he was feeling.

"Did you ever discuss this later in your life with her?"

"No, of course not. She wouldn't have believed it even if I had done. She always thought that the British school system was the best and that I was just a reacting to a regime that everybody else's son had gone through and survived. I turned against them both, and I will never forget the anger I felt when she said I was to get on with life, and to rise above it and then they went off to live in sunny Jamaica with all the rich people."

His contempt was obvious. But they had retired after a life of work. Some had inherited I guess but the others had worked for it. I wonder if he knew how hard people do work, it is the consistency of it, the day-to-day struggles, the sacrifices that parents make when they have children. They have to think twice about their own enjoyment and budget especially if they are planning to send their children to private schools and University. It takes years of slogging to save that kind of money and if you have no help from any member of the immediate family, it takes a great deal of effort. So when you manage to achieve these things for your children you expect them to do well. I suppose Charles's mother hated to send him away and probably missed him more than he missed her as he was busier at school than she was at home.

I listened to his angry words and wondered how and when he would recover from this trauma. It was difficult to know what to say when he finally stopped talking.

I paid the bill, and we walked out as the traffic roared by.

"I expect you are shocked at my reactions when these things happened so long ago."

We walked towards Oxford Street around Soho Square.

"No, I am very pleased you told me how you feel. It all falls into place now. I will have to think about what you have told me and I do understand now what you went through."

"Dad knows it really, and I am waiting to see what he does next. When your parents just ignore your pleas you begin not to trust them anymore."

"Now that we have got to know each other better, do you think the three of us could go out sometime together?" I asked.

"I guess so. So you and Dad are a number are you? I think that's hysterical, you and Dad. At least he didn't run off with a dumb redhead. Better you than anyone, I'd say."

"Well, thanks very much. I take that as a compliment."

"I hope you can make Dad understand how I feel." He looked at me as we turned the corner.

"Of course. Honestly Charles, he loves you very very much and now we are kind of starting off a new phase of our lives, it would be wonderful if you would be part of it."

"Do you think that is possible, after all the bad things we have said to each other?"

"Of course. It is never too late. If you stay here in London I could introduce you to some of my friends. I think you would like them especially the musicians I know."

"Like who?"

"Like Elton John, Phil Collins, Sting….."

"Really?"

"No I'm joking. I don't know them but I have friends who do."

"I am upset about Stan and the group, but they are so changeable they never know what they are doing. I'm fed up with them all."

"What will you do then?"

"Get another job, I guess."

"We would love you to be with us more. I know your Dad would love it."

We spent more time discussing his music and how he wanted to play music rather than go to University and get further training.

He was almost obsessed by it and I knew that he would have to work at it and then see how things panned out. If Nigel wanted to become friends then we would have to realize this together.

When Nigel and I married, he came to the wedding, which was nice of him, and it wasn't till months afterwards, that we had such a fight.

When I told all this to Henry, I was rather annoyed when he didn't comment.

"So was I wrong to leave?"

He still wouldn't say much except that he wanted to be let out of the argument. "No advice then?"

"Much too complicated Nicole. You know I used to be a school teacher."

"Oh yes of course. So you go with the classical education?"

"Not always. In this day and age there is the digital world out there. If you are good with computers and know the business, then perhaps a classical education is not necessary."

I thought of my girlfriend's son, he was brilliant. He was a computer programmer and was making pots of money. He hadn't even finished high school. I don't know what to think.

"I just feel Nigel is a bit obsessed with it all."

But then when Nigel came to London Charles became really unmanageable. One day we were all walking in the park, and I said something about Charles wanting to become a musician, giving him a little support I thought, then Nigel flew at me. He completely snapped. Maybe it was jet lag or something. But Charles witnessed the whole thing.

"Stay out of this Nicole, he is not your son!"

I was devastated and hurt. I couldn't stay with them, and just turned on my heel and left them to it. It was then I knew I had to try to get a new life, and I came down here.

Next day I closed up my flat, and left.

Chapter Thirteen

The house was nearly finished. It was rather stressful to go up day after day and wait to see if everything was where I had planned things to go. The news was out, I don't know how, but real estate agents started phoning me. I knew that Jean and Marie must have told a few people, but I was irritated because I still haven't decided what to do with the house. I was certain that when the winter came, it would be too cold to live there. Even with the heating put in, the house itself wasn't insulated well enough.

When I got back to the *pension* that evening, I was rather depressed at the whole situation. My writing was not going well and I felt that I hadn't achieved very much at all. I hadn't figured out whether it was more miserable to be miserable in a foreign country than be miserable back home.

When Nigel showed up one day I was dumbfounded. He had kept his promise that he wouldn't try to contact me and I had only kept in touch by a few e mails to say that I was managing and was not in any difficulties, as he said he needed to know that.

It was a bit like Shirley Valentine at the end of the film, when her husband shows up in Greece, and she invites him to sit down and have a drink with her in the sunset. I was sitting as usual, at the Carlton, on the terrace, and suddenly there he was. I think I must have told him that I loved that place. However in the film, what happens? You never find out. Does Shirley go back home with him or not? Do we want to know? I think every woman wants to know. But why didn't the playwright tell us?

This wonderful Riviera is inspiring but when it all comes down to the reality of living, having someone you love is the most important thing in life I decided.

It was Noel Coward who wrote that love was all, and when he was interviewed towards the end of his life, he still said the same thing. I knew that Nigel loved me and I was a fool to think I could live alone down here in my cottage. We could sort out his son's problems together. Staying in France was unrealistic; my French wasn't good enough for one thing! We could keep the little cottage for holidays and stay for longer over the summer. Nigel had apologized for his outburst and I knew he was hoping we would try again. I have enough material now, to finish writing the book back in England.

I took him up to see the cottage and he was delighted with it, especially the fantastic view.

A few days later we left for London. I said goodbye to Henry who thought I was doing the right thing, even though he said he would miss me very much. My sojourn was over but I knew we would return. I phoned Pauline and explained what happened; we said we would keep in touch. Julia had just left for her exhibition in Paris, so I would write to her later. She had inspired me so much, I knew I would never forget her and her dedication to her work. I wondered if anyone would realize how difficult it had been for her, to move to France and continue her work.

I was sad to be leaving and knew I would miss this glorious place. But the Riviera would always be there, maybe one day when Nigel retires. In the meantime it was a goal to become fluent in French for whenever that day came, and to remember at least I gave it a try and now there were other people who needed me. Nigel and Charles. I realized that they were more important right now than the ghosts of the past.

We will come back and stay in the little cottage periodically, and hopefully Henry will come and visit us in Oxford. I might even find him a wife, who would be delighted to change her life and go and live on the Riviera, even maybe a write book! In fact, I just thought someone, who would suit perfectly!

The End

www.sharland.com